Pierre Souvestre, Marcel Allain

The Exploits of Juve: Fantômas Saga

OK Publishing 2021

Pierre Souvestre, Marcel Allain
The Exploits of Juve: Fantômas Saga

Published by
MUSAICUM
Books

- Advanced Digital Solutions & High-Quality book Formatting -

musaicumbooks@okpublishing.info

2021 OK Publishing

ISBN 978-80-272-7885-5

Contents

I
THE COMRADES' TRYST

"A bowl of claret, Father Korn."

The raucous voice of big Ernestine rose above the hubbub in the smoke-begrimed tavern.

"Some claret, and let it be good," repeated the drab, a big, fair damsel with puckered eyes and features worn by dissipation.

Father Korn had heard the first time, but he was in no hurry to comply with the order.

He was a bald, whiskered giant, and at the moment was busily engaged in swilling dirty glasses in a sink filled with tepid water.

This tavern, "The Comrades' Tryst," had two rooms, each with its separate exit. Mme. Korn presided over the first in which food and drink were served. By passing through the door at the far end, and crossing the inner courtyard of the large seven-story building, the second "den" was reached — a low and ill-lit room facing the Rue de la Charbonnière, a street famed in the district for its bad reputation.

At a third summons, Father Korn, who had sized up the girl and the crowd she was with, growled:

"It'll be two moons; hand over the stuff first."

Big Ernestine rose, and pushing her way to him, began a long argument. When she stopped to draw a breath, Korn interposed:

"It's no use trying that game. I said two francs and two francs it is."

"All right, I won't argue with a brute like you," replied the girl. "Everyone knows that you and Mother Korn are Germans, dirty Prussians."

The innkeeper smiled quietly and went on washing his glasses.

Big Ernestine glanced around the room. She knew the crowd and quickly decided that the cash would not be forthcoming.

For a moment she thought of tackling old Mother Toulouche, ensconced in the doorway with her display of portugals and snails, but dame Toulouche, snuggled in her old shawl, was fast asleep.

Suddenly from a corner of the tavern, a weary voice cried with authority:

"Go ahead, Korn, I'll stand treat."

It was the Sapper who had spoken.

A man of fifty who owed his nickname to the current report that he had spent twenty years in Africa, both as a soldier and a convict.

While Ernestine and her friends hastened to his table, the Sapper's companion, a heavily built man, rose carelessly and slouched off to join another group, muttering:

"I'm too near the window here."

"It's Nonet," explained the Sapper to Ernestine. "He's home from New Caledonia, and he doesn't care to show himself much just now."

The girl nodded, and pointing to one of her companions, became confidential. "Look at poor Mimile, here. He's just out of quod and has to start right off to do his service. Pretty tough."

The Sapper became very interested in the conversation. Meanwhile Nonet, as he crossed the tap-room, had stopped a few moments before a pretty girl who was evidently expecting some one.

"Waiting again for the Square, eh, Josephine?" Nonet inquired.

The girl, whose big blue eyes contrasted strikingly with her jet black hair, replied:

"Why not? Loupart doesn't think of quitting me that I know of."

"Well, when he does let me know," Nonet suggested smilingly.

Josephine shrugged her shoulders contemptuously, and, glancing at the clock above the bar, rose suddenly and left the tap-room.

She went rapidly down the Rue Charbonnière and along the boulevard, in the direction of the Barbès Metropolitan Station. On reaching the level of the Boulevard Magenta, she slackened and walked along the right-hand pavement toward the centre of Paris.

"My little Jojo!"

The girl who, after leaving the tavern, had assumed a quiet and modest air, now came face to face with a stout gentleman with a jovial face and one gleaming eye, the other eye being permanently closed. He wore a beard turning grey and his derby hat and light cane placed him as belonging to the middle class.

"How late you are, my adored Jojo," he murmured tenderly. "That accursed workshop been keeping you again after hours?"

The mistress of Loupart checked a smile.

"That's it!" she replied, "the workshop, M. Martialle."

The man addressed made a warning gesture.

"Don't mention my name here; I'm almost home." He pulled out his watch. "Too bad; I'll have to go in or my wife will kick up a row. Let's see, this is Tuesday; well, Saturday I'm off to Burgundy on my usual half-monthly trip. Meet me at the Lyons station, platform No. 2, Marseilles express. We won't be back till Monday. A delightful week-end of love-making with my darling who at last consents....What's that!"

The stout man broke off his impassioned harangue. A beggar, emerging from the darkness, importuned him:

"Have pity on me, kind sir."

"Give him something," urged Josephine.

The middle-aged lover complied and tenderly drew away the pretty girl, repeating carefully the details of the assignation:

"Lyons Station; a quarter past eight. The train leaves at twenty to nine."

Then suddenly dropping Josephine's arm:

"Now, sweetheart, you'd better hurry home to your good mother, and remember Saturday."

The outline of the portly personage faded into the night. Loupart's mistress shrugged her shoulders, turned, and made her way back to the "Tryst," where her place had been kept for her.

At the back of the tavern, the group which Nonet had joined were discussing strange doings. "The Bear," head of the band of the Cyphers, had just returned from the courthouse. He brought the latest news. Riboneau had been given ten years, but was going to try for a reduced sentence.

The talk suddenly dropped. A hubbub arose outside, a dull roar which waxed louder and louder. The sound of hurrying footsteps mingled with shrill cries and oaths. Doors in the street slammed. A few shots were fired, followed by a pause, and then the stampede began again.

Father Korn, deserting his bar, warily planted himself at the entry to his establishment, his hand on the latch of the door. He stood ready to bar entrance to any who might try to press in.

"The raid," he warned in a low tone.

His customers, glad to feel themselves in safety, followed the vicissitudes of what to them was almost a daily occurrence.

First came the frenzied rush of the "street walkers," deserted by their sinister protectors and fleeing madly in search of shelter in terror of the lock-up. Behind the shrieking herd the constables, in close ranks, swept and cleared the street, leaving no corner, no court, no door that remained ajar unsearched. Then the whirl swept away, the noise died down, and the street resumed its normal aspect: drab, weird and alarming.

Father Korn laughed. "All they've bagged is Bonzville!" he cried, and the customers responded to his merriment. The police had been fooled again. Bonzville was a harmless old tramp, who got himself "jugged" every winter on purpose to lay up for repairs.

The passage of the "driver" had caused enough stir in the tap-room to distract attention from the entry at the back of a stoutly built man with a bestial face, known by the title of "The Cooper."

Swiftly he passed to the Beard's table, and, taking the latter aside, began:

"The big job is fixed for the end of the week. On my way back from the station I saw Josephine palavering with the swell customer...."

Suddenly the Beard stopped him short.

The general attention had become fixed on the street entrance to the tap-room. The door had opened with a bang and Loupart, alias "The Square," the popular lover of the pretty Josephine, came on the scene, his eyes gleaming, his lips smiling under his upturned moustache.

Then there broke out cries of stupefaction. Loupart was between two policemen, who had stopped short in the doorway.

The Square turned to them: "Thank you, gentlemen," he said in his most urbane tone. "I am very grateful to you for having seen me this far. I am quite safe now. Let me offer you a drink to the health of authority!"

However, the two policemen did not dare to enter the tavern, so they briefly declined and made off. Josephine had risen, and Loupart, after pressing a tender kiss upon her lips, turned to the company.

"That feazes you, eh! I was just heading this way when I ran into the drive. As I'm a peaceful citizen, I got hold of two cops and begged them to see me safely home. They thought I was really scared."

There was a burst of general laughter. No one could bluff the police like the Square.

Loupart turned to Josephine: "How are things going, ducky?"

The girl repeated in a low tone to her lover her recent talk with M. Martialle.

Loupart nodded approvingly, but grumbled when he found the meeting was fixed for Saturday.

"Hang the fellow! Must hustle with all the jobs on hand this week. Anyway, we won't let this one slip by. Plenty of shiners, eh, Josephine?"

"You bet. He carries the stuff to his partners every fortnight."

"That's first rate, but in the meantime there's something doing to-night. Here, kiddy, take a pen and scratch off a letter for me."

The Square dictated in a low voice:

"Sir, I am only a poor girl, but I've some feeling and honesty and I hate to see wrong done around me. Believe me, you'd better keep an eye open on some one pretty close to me. Maybe the police have already told you I am the mistress of Loupart, alias the Square. I'm not denying it; in fact, I'm proud of it. Well, I swear to you that this Loupart is going to try a dirty game."

Josephine stopped writing.

"Look here, what are you at?"

"Scribble, and don't bother yourself. This doesn't concern you," replied Loupart drily.

Josephine waited, docile and ready, but the Square's attention was now focussed upon Ernestine, her young man and the generous Sapper.

"Yes," Ernestine was explaining to Mimile while the Sapper nodded approvingly, "the Beard is, as you might say, the head of the band of Cyphers, next to Loupart, of course. To belong to the Beard's gang you've got to have done up at least one guy. Then you get your Number 1. Your figure increases according to the number of deaders you have to your credit."

"So then," inquired Mimile, with eager curiosity, "Riboneau, who has just been sentenced, is called number 'seven' because ..."

"Because," added the Sapper in his serious voice, "because he has killed off seven."

In a few curt questions the Square posted himself as to young Mimile, who had impressed him favourably.

Josephine turned to Loupart: "What else am I to put in the letter? Why are you stopping?"

For answer, the Square suddenly sprang to his feet, seized a half-empty bottle and flung it on the floor, where it broke. This act of violence sent the company scattering, and Loupart roared out:

"It's on account of spies that I'm stopping! By God! When are we going to see their finish? And besides," he added, staring hard at Ernestine, "I've had enough of all this nonsense; better clear out of here or there'll be trouble."

Cunningly, with bloodshot eyes, her fists clenched in fury, but humbly submissive, the girl made ready to comply. She knew the Square was master, and there was no use standing out against his will.

The Sapper himself, growling, picked up his change, little disposed to have a row, and beckoning to his comrade, Nonet, effected a humble exit under cover of the girl Ernestine.

Loupart's arm fell upon the shoulder of Mimile, who alone seemed to defy Josephine's formidable lover.

"Hold on, young 'un," ordered Loupart. "You seem to have some nerve; better join us."

Mimile's eyes lighted up with joy.

"Oh!" he stammered, "Loupart, you'll take me in the Cypher gang?"

"Maybe," was the enigmatic reply. Then with a shove he sent the young man to the back of the den. "Must go and talk it over with the Beard." Without paying heed to the thanks of his new recruit, Loupart continued his dictation to Josephine.

As the Sapper and Nonet went quickly down the Rue Charbonnière, Nonet inquired:

"Well, chief, what do you think of our evening?"

The individual that the hooligans of La Chapelle knew by the nickname of the Sapper, and who was no other than Inspector Michel, slowly stroked his long beard:

"Not much," he declared, "except that we've been bluffed by the Square."

"Why not round up the bunch?" suggested Nonet, who was known as Inspector Léon.

"It's easy enough to talk, but what can two do against twenty? Who wants to take such risks for sixty dollars a month?"

In the meantime Josephine was writing at the Square's dictation:

"I know, sir, that to-morrow Loupart will be at Garnet's wine-shop at seven o'clock, which you know is to the right as you go up the Faubourg Montmartre, before you reach the Rue Lamartine. From there he will go to Doctor Chaleck's to tackle the safe, which is placed, as I told you, at the far side of the study, facing the window, with its balcony overlooking the garden. I wouldn't have meddled in the matter except that there'll be something worse regarding a woman. I can't tell you any more, for this is all I know. Make the best of it, and for God's sake never let Loupart know the letter was sent to you by the undersigned.

"Very respectfully,"

About to sign her name, Josephine looked up, trembling and anxious.

"What does it mean, Loupart? You've been drinking, I'm sure you have!"

"Sign, I tell you," calmly replied the Square, and the girl, hypnotised, proceeded to trace in her large clumsy hand, her name, "Josephine Ramot."

"Now put it in an envelope."

From the end of the saloon the Beard was signalling Loupart.

"What is it?" the latter cried, annoyed at the interruption.

The Beard came near and whispered:

"Important business. The dock man's scheme is going well — it'll be for the end of the week, Saturday at latest."

"In four days, then?"

"In four days."

"All right," declared Josephine's lover, "we'll be on hand. It'll be a big haul, I hear."

"Fifty thousand at least, the Cooper told me."

Loupart nodded, waved the Beard aside and resumed:

"Address it to

"Monsieur Juve,

"Commissioner of Safety,

"At the Prefecture, Paris."

II

ON THE TRACK

The daily paper, *The Capital*, was about to go to press. The editors had handed over the last slips of copy with the latest news.

"Well, Fandor," asked the Secretary, "nothing more for me?"

"No, nothing."

"You won't spring a 'latest' on me?"

"Not unless the President of the Republic should be assassinated."

"Right enough. But don't joke. Lord, there's something else to be done just now."

The "setter up" appeared in the editor's rooms:

"I want sharp type for 'one,' and eight lines for 'two.'"

Discreetly, as a man accustomed to the business, Fandor withdrew on hearing the request of the "setter up," avoiding the searching glance of the sub-editor, who forthwith to meet the demands of the paging, called at random one of the reporters and passed on the order to him.

"Some lines of special type; eight lines. Take up the Cretan question on the Havas telegrams. Be quick!"

Fandor picked up his hat and stick and left the office. His berth as police-reporter meant a constantly active and unsettled existence. He was never his own master, never knew ten minutes beforehand what he was going to do, whether he might go home, start on a journey, interview a minister or risk his life by an investigation in the world of thugs and cut-throats.

"Deuce take it!" he cried as he passed the office door and saw what the time was. "I simply must go to the courts, and it's already very late...." He ran forward a few paces, then stopped short. "And that porter murdered at Belleville!...If I don't cover that affair I shall have nothing interesting to turn in...."

He retraced his steps, looking for a cab and swearing at the narrowness of the Rue Montmartre, where the inadequate pavements forced the foot passengers to overflow on to the roadway, which was choked with costermongers' carts, heavy motor-buses, and all that swarm of vehicles which gives a Paris street an air of bustle unequalled in any other capital in the world. As he was about to pass the corner of the Rue Bergère, a porter laden down with sample boxes, strung on a hook, ran into him, almost knocking him down.

"Look where you're going!" cried the journalist.

"Look out yourself," replied the man insolently.

Fandor, with an angry shrug of his shoulders, was about to pursue his way, when the man stopped him.

"Sir, can you direct me to the Rue du Croissant?"

"Follow the Rue Montmartre and take the second turning to the right."

"Thank you, sir; could you give me a light?"

Fandor could not repress a smile. He held out his cigarette. "Here; is that all you want to-day?"

"Well, you might offer me a drink."

Fandor was about to answer sharply when something in the man's face seemed vaguely familiar. He was about sixty. His clothes were threadbare and green with age, his shoes down at the heels, his moustache and shaggy beard a dirty yellow.

"Why the devil should I stand you a drink?"

"A good impulse, M. Fandor."

In a moment the man's features seemed to change. He appeared quite a different person and Fandor recognised who was speaking to him. Accustomed by long habit to conceal his impressions, the journalist spoke nonchalantly:

"All right; let's go to the 'Grand Charlemagne.'"

They started off together, reached the Faubourg Montmartre and entered a small wine-shop. Having taken their seats and ordered drinks, Fandor turned to the porter.

"What's up?" he asked.

"It takes you a long time to recognise your friends."

Fandor scrutinised his companion.

"You are wonderfully made up, Juve."

On hearing his name mentioned, the man gave a start. "Don't utter my name! They know me here as old Paul."

"But why the disguise? Who are you after? Is it anything to do with Fantômas?"

Juve shrugged his shoulders. "Let's leave Fantômas out of it," he said. "At least for the moment. No, my lad, it's a very commonplace affair to-day, and I wouldn't have bumped into you except that I have an hour to while away and wanted your company."

"This disguise for a commonplace affair?" cried Fandor. "Come, Juve, don't keep me in the dark."

Juve laughed at his friend's eagerness.

"You'll always be the same. When it's a matter of detective work, there's no keeping you out of it. Well, here's the information you're after. Read that."

He passed Fandor a greasy, ill-written letter. Fandor took it in at a glance.

"This refers to Loupart, alias the Square?"

"Yes."

"And you call it a commonplace affair? But, look here, can you trust information given by a loose woman?"

"My dear Fandor, the police largely depend upon such tips, given through revenge by women of that class."

"Well, I'm going with you."

"No, I won't have you mixed up in this business; it's too dangerous."

"All the more reason for my being in it! What is really known about this Loupart?"

"Very little, unfortunately," rejoined Juve. "And it's the mystery surrounding him which makes us uneasy. Although he has been involved in some of the worst crimes, he has always managed to escape arrest. He is supposed to be one of an organised gang. In any case, he's a resolute scoundrel who wouldn't hesitate to draw his gun in case of need."

Fandor nodded.

"His arrest will make bully copy."

"And for the pleasure of writing a sensational story you want to put your life in peril again!" Juve smiled sympathetically as he spoke. He had known the young journalist, when, scarcely grown up, he had been involved in the weird affairs of "Fantômas."

Fandor was an assumed name. Juve recalled the young Charles Rambert, victim of the mysterious Fantômas, the most redoubtable ruffian of modern times, whom Juve declared to be Gurn and still alive, although Gurn had supposedly died on the scaffold. He recalled the sensational trial and the terrible revelations that had appalled society. Gurn he had then affirmed to be the lover of the Englishwoman, Lady Beltham. Gurn it was who had killed her husband, and Gurn was no other than Fantômas.

He recalled the tragical morning when Gurn, in the very shadow of the scaffold, had found means to send in his stead an innocent victim, Valgrand, the actor.

"When will you begin to draw in your net?" inquired Fandor.

Juve motioned to his companion to be silent and listen.

"Fandor, you hear what that man's singing; the one drinking at the bar?"

"Yes, 'The Blue Danube.'"

"Well, that gives me the answer. We shall soon be on Loupart's tracks. By the way, are you armed?"

"If you won't run me in for carrying concealed weapons I'll confess that Baby Browning is in my pocket."

"Good. Now, then, listen to my directions. Loupart was seen at the markets this morning by two of my watchers, and you may be sure he hasn't been lost sight of since. Reports I have received indicate that he will presumably go to the Chateaudun cross-roads and from there to the Place Pigalle, in the direction of Doctor Chaleck's house. We shall nab him at the cross-roads. Needless to say we are not going to keep together. As soon as our man comes in sight you will pass on ahead, walking at his pace on the same pavement and without turning round."

"And if Loupart doesn't appear?"

"Why then — " began Juve. "The deuce! There's another customer whistling 'The Blue Danube.' It's time to be off."

"Are those your agents whistling?" asked Fandor, as they left the shop.

"No."

"What! Isn't it a signal?"

"It is, and you'll be able to find your trail by the passers-by who whistle that air."

While talking, the journalist and the detective arrived at the Chateaudun cross-roads. Juve cast an eye over the ground.

"It's six o'clock. Be off and prowl around Notre Dame de Lorette. Loupart will probably come out of that wine-shop you see to the right. You can easily recognise him by his height and a scar on his left cheek."

"Look here, Juve, why should these people whistle 'The Blue Danube' if they are not detectives?"

Juve smiled. "It's quite simple. If you whistle a popular tune in a crowd, some one is bound to take it up. Well, the two men I put to watching Loupart this morning were whistling this same tune, and now we are meeting persons who caught the air."

Fandor crossed the road and proceeded toward Notre Dame de Lorette to the post the detective had allotted to him. The man hunt was about to begin.

III
BEHIND THE CURTAIN

The Cité Frochot is shut in by low stone walls, topped by grating round which creepers intertwine.

The entry to its main thoroughfare, shaded by trees and lined with small private houses, is not supposed to be public, and a porter's lodge to the right of the entrance is intended to enforce its private character.

It was about seven in the evening. As the fine spring day drew to a close, Fandor reached the square of the Cité. For an hour past the journalist had been wholly engaged in keeping track of the famous Loupart, who, after leaving the saloon, had sauntered up the Rue des Martyrs, his hands in his pockets and a cigarette in his mouth.

Fandor allowed him to pass at the corner of the Rue Claude, and from there on kept him in view.

Juve had completely disappeared.

As Loupart, followed by Fandor, was about to enter the Cité Frochot, an exclamation made them both turn.

Fandor perceived a poorly dressed man anxiously searching for something in the gutter. A curious crowd had instantly collected, and word was passed round that the lost object was a twenty-five-franc gold piece.

Fandor, joining the crowd, was pushed close to the man, who quickly whispered:

"Idiot! Keep out of the Cité."

The owner of the gold piece was no other than the detective. Then, under cover of loud complaint, Juve muttered to Fandor, "Let him go! Watch the entrance to the Cité!"

"But," objected Fandor in the same key, "what if I lose sight of him?"

"No fear of that. The doctor's house is the second on the right." The hooligan, who had for a moment drawn near the crowd, was now heading straight for the Cité.

Juve went on: "In a quarter of an hour at the latest join me again, 27 Rue Victor Massé."

"And if Loupart should enter the Cité in the meantime?"

"Come straight back to me."

Fandor was moving off when Juve addressed him out loud: "Thank you, kind gentlemen! But as you are so charitable, give me something more for God's sake."

The other drew near the pretended beggar and Juve added:

"If anyone questions you as you pass through, say you are going to Omareille, the decorator's; you'll find me on the stairs."

Some moments later the little crowd had melted away and a policeman, arriving as usual too late, wondered what had been going on.

Fandor carried out Juve's instructions to the letter. Hiding behind a sentry box he kept an eye on the doctor's house, but nothing out of the way happened. Loupart had vanished, although he was probably not far away. When the fifteen minutes were up Fandor left his post and entered No. 27 Rue Victor Massé. As he reached the third floor he heard Juve's voice:

"Is that you, lad?"

"Yes."

"The porter didn't question you?"

"I've seen no one."

"All right, come up here."

Juve was seated at a hall window examining Doctor Chaleck's house through a field glass.

"You've not seen Loupart go in?" he inquired as Fandor joined him.

"Not while I was on watch."

"It's well to know one's Paris and have friends everywhere, isn't it?" continued Juve. "It occurred to me quite suddenly that this might be an excellent place from where to follow citizen

Loupart's doings. You would have spoiled everything if you had followed him into the Cité. That's why I devised my little scheme to hold you back."

"You are right," admitted Fandor, who, the next moment, gave a jump as Juve's hand gripped him hard.

"Look, Fandor! The bird is going into the cage!"

The journalist, excited, saw a figure already familiar to him in the act of slipping into the little garden which separated Dr. Chaleck's house from the main thoroughfare.

The detective went on: "There he goes, skirting the house until he reaches the little door hidden in the wall. What's he up to now? Ah! He's fumbling in his pocket. False keys, of course."

They saw Loupart open the door and make his way into the house.

"What comes next?" inquired Fandor.

"We are going to tighten the net which the silly bird has hopped into," rejoined Juve, as he bolted down the stairs, and added as a precautionary measure: "While I question the porter, you slip by me into the main street. I have every reason to believe that M. Chaleck has been absent for two days, and as soon as I get this information, I shall pretend to go away, and then — the rest is my concern."

Juve's program was carried out in all points.

To his questions, the porter replied:

"Why, sir, I can't really say. I saw Doctor Chaleck go off with his bag and I haven't seen him come back. However, if you care to see for yourself — — "

"No, thanks," replied Juve, "I'll return in a few days. But look out, your lamp's flaring!"

As the porter turned to remedy the trouble, Juve, instead of going off to the right, quickly followed the direction Fandor had taken and caught up with the latter just outside Doctor Chaleck's house.

"Now for our plan of campaign," he said. "It's darker now than it will be later when the street lamps are lit and the moon rises. That excellent Josephine sent me a rough plan of the house. You see there are two windows on the ground floor on either side of the hall. Naturally they belong to the dining-room and drawing-room. The window to the right on the first floor is evidently that of the bedroom. On the left, this window with a balcony belongs to the study of our dealer in death! That's where we must plant ourselves. Understand, Fandor?"

The journalist nodded. "I understand."

The two men advanced carefully, holding their breath and halting at every step. To catch the ruffian in the act they must reach the study without giving the alarm.

The first story of Doctor Chaleck's house was only slightly raised above the ground: by the aid of a drain-pipe Juve and Fandor managed without difficulty to hoist themselves on to the balcony.

"Here's luck," cried Juve. "The study window is wide open!"

After putting on a pair of rubbers and making Fandor remove his boots, the two men entered the room. Juve's first precaution was to test the two halves of the window. Finding that their hinges did not creak, he fastened the latch and drew the curtains.

"We'll risk a light," he whispered, taking out a pocket-lamp, which lit up the room sufficiently to allow him to take his bearings.

The study was elegantly furnished. In the middle was a huge desk piled with papers, reports, and files. To the right of the desk in the corner opposite the window and half hidden by a heavy velvet curtain was the door leading to the landing. A large corner sofa occupied the space of two wall panels. A set of book-shelves covered a whole wall. Here and there cosy armchairs invited meditation.

"I don't see the famous safe," Murmured Fandor.

"That's because your eyes aren't trained," replied the detective. "Look at that corner sofa, topped by that richly carved bracket. Observe the thick appearance of the delicate mahogany panel. You may be quite sure that it hides a solid steel casket which the best tools would have no easy job to cut through. That little moulding you see to the right can be easily pushed aside."

Here Juve, with the precision of an expert, set the woodwork in motion and showed the astonished Fandor a scarcely visible key-hole.

"Now, let's put out the light and hide ourselves behind the curtains. Luckily they are far enough from the window for our presence not to be noticed."

For about an hour the men remained motionless, then, weary of standing, they squatted on the floor. Each had his revolver ready to hand.

Ten had just struck from a distant clock when suddenly a slight sound reached their attentive ears.

The two had whiled away the time of waiting by drilling the curtains with a small penknife. These holes were invisible at a distance, but enabled them to see what was going on in the room.

The noise continued, slow and measured; some one was walking about in the adjacent rooms without any attempt to disguise the sound. Evidently Loupart believed himself quite alone in the house of the absent doctor.

The steps drew nearer, and Fandor, in spite of his courage, felt the rapid beating of his heart. The handle of the door leading from the hall to the study was turned, and some person entered the room.

There was an instant of silence, and then the desk was suddenly lit up. The new-comer had found the switch. But he was not Loupart.

He seemed a man of forty and wore a brown beard, brushed fan-shape; a noticeable baldness heightened his forehead. On his strongly arched nose a double eye-glass was balanced. Suddenly, having looked at the clock which marked half-past eleven, he began to loosen his tie and unbutton his waistcoat and then went out, leaving the study lit as if intending to come back.

"It's Chaleck!" exclaimed Fandor.

"Just so," replied the detective. "And this complicates matters; we may have to protect him as well as his safe."

Indeed, Juve's first impulse was to go straight to Doctor Chaleck, apprise him of the situation, and, under his guidance, search the house thoroughly. But that would have put Loupart on the alert. It would be taking too great a chance. If Juve should lay hands on him outside of Chaleck's house he would have no right to hold him. For the subtle power of Loupart, that well-loved hooligan of the purlieus of Paris, lay in his remaining constantly a source of fear, always a suspect without ever being caught with the goods.

Coming back to his first idea of insuring Chaleck's safety, Juve said to himself: "The doctor is coming back here, that's sure, and we must protect him without his knowing it. That is the best plan for the present."

Sure enough after an absence of ten minutes Chaleck returned to the study and seated himself at his desk. He had now changed into his pajamas.

Time passed.

When the little Empire time piece which decorated the mantel struck three, Fandor, for all his anxiety, could not repress a yawn: the night was long and thus far had been devoid of incidents. From their hiding-place, he and Juve kept an eye on Doctor Chaleck. When did the man sleep?

Nothing in the physician's countenance betrayed the slightest weariness. He examined numerous documents spread out on the desk, and also wrote a letter which he sealed by lighting a candle and melting some wax. He lingered a good twenty minutes afterwards, then finally put out the lights and left the room.

The room was now in total darkness. The journalist and the detective listened a few moments longer as a precaution, but nothing happened to break the hush of the waning night.

Half an hour more and the outlines of the two would be visible on the thin curtains. It was high time to be off.

Fandor and Juve rose with difficulty to their feet, so cramped were their legs from the enforced rigidity.

"What now?" asked Fandor.

"Listen!" Juve abruptly gripped the other's arm as a fresh noise came to their ears. This time it was not the footsteps of a man walking carelessly, but weird creakings, sly gropings. The noise stopped, began again and again stopped. Where did it come from?

"This room is a mass of hangings," muttered Juve.

"It's impossible to locate those sounds or determine their origin."

"You would suppose," began Fandor — —

But he stopped short. The door had opened, the light was switched on and Doctor Chaleck appeared once more, probably disturbed in his sleep by the mysterious noises.

Chaleck gave a quick glance round the room, and then, to the consternation of the two men, he took a few steps toward the window, revolver in hand. At this moment dull creakings were heard, apparently coming from the landing. Chaleck turned quickly, and, leaving the door open, went out. An increase of light indicated that the other rooms in the house were being searched, and as the lights were gradually switched off again, it was apparent that Chaleck was concluding his domiciliary visit without having noticed anything abnormal.

The two remained still for an hour longer, although they had heard Chaleck go back to his room and lock himself into it.

Meantime the daylight was growing brighter, and in a little while the neighbourhood would be awake.

"We must slip out," decreed Juve, as he turned the hasp of the window with infinite care and set it ajar to reach the balcony.

A few moments later Juve had shed his disguise and the two men drew breath in the middle of the Place Pigalle, having fled ignominiously like common criminals.

IV
A WOMAN'S CORPSE

"Well, Juve, I suppose you'll agree with me that Josephine's information was a piece of pure fiction," said Fandor as they turned into the Rue Pigalle.

"You are talking nonsense," replied Juve.

"But," protested the other, "we arrived punctually at the place appointed, and most assuredly nothing happened there."

"We were punctual, it is true, but so was Loupart. Josephine's letter gave us two items of information: That her lover would be at Doctor Chaleck's house and that he would rob the safe. Events have proved her correct in one case. As to the second, while he did not break open the safe, nothing proves that he had not that intention. He may have been frustrated by the unexpected appearance of Doctor Chaleck, or he may have discovered that we were following him."

At this moment Fandor pointed out to Juve three men who were running toward them, violently gesticulating.

"What does that mean?" he asked.

Before Juve could reply one of the men, much out of breath, inquired: "Well, chief!"

"Why, it's Michel and Henri and Léon!" Then, turning to Fandor, he explained: "Three inspectors."

Michel repeated the question: "Well, chief, what's up?"

"What do you mean?"

"You've just come from the Cité Frochot, chief?"

Juve was amazed. "Look here," he said, "where do you come from, Michel? The Prefecture?"

"No, chief, from the head office of No. IX."

"Then how do you know we were at the Cité Frochot?"

Taken aback, Michel replied: "Why, from seeing you here, after the affair."

"What affair?" insisted Juve.

"Well, chief, it's this way. The three of us were on duty this morning at the Rue Rochefoucauld Station. About twenty minutes ago the telephone rang and I heard a woman asking in a broken and choked voice if it was the police station. On my answering it was, she begged me to come to the rescue, crying, 'Murder! I'm dying!'"

"What then?" questioned Juve.

"Then I asked who was speaking, but unfortunately Central had cut me off."

"You made inquiries?"

"Yes, chief, and after a quarter of an hour Central told me that only one subscriber had called up the police station, the number being 928-12, name of Doctor Chaleck in the Cité Frochot."

"I suppose you asked for the number again?"

"I did, but I could get no reply."

After a pause, during which Juve was lost in thought, the officer added timidly: "We'd better hurry if a crime has been committed."

Juve beckoned Michel to him.

"There are too many of us," he said. "You come along, Michel; the other two must go back to the station and be ready to join us in case of need."

The two officers and Fandor went hurriedly up the Rue Pigalle and came to a halt by Doctor Chaleck's door.

A loud ringing brought no reply. It was repeated, and finally a voice cried: "Who is there; what's the matter?"

"Open," ordered Juve.

"To whom do you wish to speak?"

"To Doctor Chaleck." And Juve added: "Open, it's the police."

"The police! What the deuce do they want with me?"

"You'll soon find out," answered Michel. "Do you suppose we'd be making this row if we were criminals?"

Doubtless convinced by this reasoning, Doctor Chaleck decided at length to open his door. "What do you want with me?" he repeated.

Juve quickly explained matters.

"We've just had a telephone message to say that some ruffians, possibly murderers, are in your house."

"Murderers!" cried Chaleck in amazement. "But whom could they murder? I'm living here alone."

At this assertion, Juve, Fandor and Michel looked at each other, mystified.

"Well, in any case we must search your house from top to bottom," said Juve, and added as an afterthought: "I suppose you are thoroughly satisfied that we come with honest intentions?"

Doctor Chaleck smiled:

"Oh! Inspector Juve's features are very well known to me, and I place myself entirely at his disposition."

The three men, led by Chaleck, ransacked all the rooms on the ground floor; finding nothing suspicious, they then went up to the floor above.

"I have only three more rooms to show you, gentlemen," said the doctor. "My bathroom, my bedroom and my study."

The bathroom disclosed nothing of interest, and Chaleck, throwing open the door of another room, announced, "My study."

Scarcely had Fandor set foot in the study, from which he and Juve had so recently made their escape, when a cry burst from his lips:

"Good God! How horrible!"

The apartment was in the greatest disorder. Overturned chairs bore witness to a violent struggle. One of the mahogany panels of the desk had been partly smashed in. A window curtain was torn and hanging, and the small gas stove was broken.

Fandor, at the first glance, saw what appeared to be a long trail of blood, extending from the window to the desk. Stepping forward quickly, he discovered the body of a woman frightfully crushed and covered with blood.

"Dead some time," cried Fandor. "The body is cold and the blood already congealed."

Juve tranquilly examined the room, and took in its tragic horror. "The telephone apparatus is overturned," he muttered to himself. "There has been a struggle between the victim and the murderer. Ah! — theft was the object of the crime."

"Theft!" cried Doctor Chaleck, coming forward.

"Look, doctor, your safe has been overturned, broken in and ransacked," answered Juve, as he and Fandor cautiously lifted the woman. The body was a mass of contusions and appeared to be one large wound.

Juve turned to the doctor, who, livid with consternation, was holding up a small grey linen bag which had contained his bonds.

"Come, doctor, calm yourself and give us some information. Can you make anything of it?"

"Nothing! nothing! I heard nothing. Who is this woman? I don't know her!"

Fandor pointed to a small shoe lying in a corner.

"A fashionable woman," he said.

"Quite so," was Juve's reply, and putting his hands on Chaleck's shoulders he inquired: "A friend of yours, a mistress, eh? Come now, don't deny it."

"Deny!" protested the doctor, "deny what? You are not accusing me, are you? I know nothing of what has taken place here, and, as you see, have been robbed into the bargain."

"Is she a patient of yours?"

"I don't practise."

"A visitor, perhaps?"

"No one has been to see me to-day."

"It is not your maid?"

"No; I tell you. I am living here all by myself."

"Have you noticed this, sir?" put in Michel, as he gave Juve a handkerchief on which some vicious, greyish substance was spread in thick layers.

"Shoemakers' wax," Juve explained, after a brief glance at it. "That explains the burns we noticed. The murderer covered his victim's face with the handkerchief to prevent identification." Then, turning to Fandor, he went on in a low tone:

"But it doesn't explain how and when the crime was committed. Less than an hour ago we were in this very room, and the burgling of the safe alone would take fully an hour."

Michel, ignorant of this fact, was for arresting the doctor.

"Look here," he said sharply to Chaleck, "we've had enough yarns from you; now tell us the truth."

"But, good God! I have told you the truth!" cried Chaleck.

"And you heard nothing, although you were only a few yards away?"

"Nothing at all. I sat up working very late last night. When I went to bed, nothing had happened in the least suspicious. Oh, by the way, toward morning I did hear a slight noise. I rose and went over the house, even coming into this room. I found everything in order."

"That's a likely tale!"

"Here's a proof of what I say! When I returned to this study I used that candle and sealing wax to seal my letter, which, as you can see, is still here. Your ring at the bell awoke me not more than twenty minutes later, just as I was getting to sleep again."

"Lies!" cried Michel, turning to Juve. "Shall I arrest him?"

"The doctor is telling the truth," replied Juve, half regretfully.

Chaleck seemed very much relieved.

"Oh, you'll help me, won't you? Get me out of this abominable affair!"

As a matter of fact, Chaleck had accounted for his time with exact truthfulness.

Juve crossed the room and drew aside the curtains; upon the floor he pointed out to Fandor traces of mud. It was there that he and the journalist had stood.

"Doctor," said Juve at length, "I must ask you not to go out this morning. I am going to headquarters to ask them to send experts in anthropometry. We must photograph in detail the appearance of your study; then I will come back and make an extended inquiry and I shall want you. Michel, remain here with the doctor."

Without further words, Juve, followed by Fandor, left the house of mystery, jumped into the first cab that passed and, mopping his forehead, cried:

"It's astounding! This murder presents mysteries worthy of Fantômas himself!"

V
LOUPART'S ANGER

Loupart was taking a fruit cure. It was about ten in the morning, and along the Rues Charbonnière, Chartres and Goutte d'Or the women hawkers, driven from central Paris by the police, were making for the high ground of the populous quarters.

Loupart strolled along the pavement, making grabs at the barrows, picking a handful of strawberries or cherries as he went by. If by chance the dealer complained, she was quickly silenced by a chaffing speech or a stern glance.

The hooligan stopped at the "Comrades' Tryst," in front of which Mother Toulouche had set out a table with a large basket of winkles.

"Want to try them?" suggested the old woman on catching sight of Josephine's lover.

"Hand me a pin," he answered harshly, and in a few moments had emptied half a dozen shells.

"Friend Square, I've something to say to you."

"Out with it, then."

But before the old woman could reply, a noise of roller skates coming down the pavement made her turn.

Loupart looked round with a smile.

"Why here comes the auto-bus," he cried.

A cripple moving at a great pace came plump into the basket of shell-fish. The speed with which he travelled had earned him the nickname of the Motor. He was said to be an old railway mechanic, who had lost both legs in an accident.

"Motor," cried Mother Toulouche, "I have to be away for ten minutes or so; look after my basket, will you?"

Following the old dame to her den Loupart entered with difficulty, on account of the great quantity of heterogeneous objects with which it was crowded. The product of innumerable thefts lay heaped up pell-mell in this illicit bazaar.

Dame Toulouche, having shut the door, plunged into her subject.

"Big Ernestine is furious with you, Loupart."

"If she's threatening me," the hooligan replied, "I'll soon fix her."

"No, big Ernestine didn't want to fight, but she was annoyed at the public affront put upon her by Josephine's lover when he drove her from 'The Good Comrades' the evening before last without any reason."

"Without any reason!" growled Loupart. "Then what was her business with those spies, the Sapper and Nonet?"

"That can't be! Not the Sapper!"

"Spies, I tell you; they belong to headquarters."

The old receiver of stolen goods cast up her eyes. "And they looked such decent people, too! Who can one trust?"

Loupart, for reply, suddenly picked up a scarf pin set with a diamond, and, tossing the old Woman a five-dollar piece, said as he left the room: "You can tell Ernestine that I bear her no malice."

Loupart had hardly gone a few steps along the Rue Charbonnière, when, at the corner of the Rue de Chartres, he bumped into a passer-by who was coming down the street.

Loupart burst out laughing: "What! Can this be you, Beard? What's happened to you?"

It certainly needed a practised eye to recognise the famous leader of the Cypher gang. For the Beard, who owed his name to an abnormal hairy development, was clean shaved; in addition, he wore a soft, greenish hat and was clad in a suit with huge checks.

"You told me to make up as an American."

"I did, and you've made yourself look like a hayseed juggins. For Heaven's sake, take it off. By the way, what about young Mimile?"

"He's with us."

"Well, get him the togs of a collegian for the job at the docks. What night do we bring it off?"

"Saturday night, unless the Cooper changes the time."

Loupart bent close to the ear of his lieutenant.

"Is he — easy to recognise?"

"No chance of making an error. Lean, togged in dark clothes and with one goggle eye."

Loupart touched the "Beard's" arm.

"First-class tickets for everybody."

"How many will there be?"

"Five or six."

"Women, too?"

"No, only my girl. But you can bet we shan't be bored!" With these words, Loupart walked away. He stopped a little later at the second house in the Rue Goutte d'Or, a decent-looking house with carpet on the stairs.

On reaching the fifth floor, he knocked several times on the door facing him, but without reply. This annoyed him; he didn't like Josephine to sleep late, and he expected her to be always ready when he condescended to come and fetch her.

Josephine was a pretty burnisher from Belleville, and Loupart, who had met her at a ball in that quarter six months ago had made her his favourite mistress.

Among the bullies and drabs that frequented the place, Josephine had appeared to him seductive, charming, almost virginal, and the popular hooligan had promptly chosen her from her sisters of the underworld.

Certainly Josephine had no reason to complain of her lover's conduct, and if at times he demanded of her a blind submission, he never treated her with that fierce brutality which characterised most of his fellows. But if Josephine had felt any leaning toward a good life, or any scruples of conscience, she must necessarily have thrown them overboard as soon as her connection with Loupart began. With a different start in life she might have become an honest little woman, but circumstances made her the mistress of a hooligan ring-leader, and, everything considered, she had a certain pride in being so, without imitating the vulgar and brutal behaviour of her companions.

At the third summons, Loupart, none too patient, drove the door in with a vigorous shove of his shoulders.

Josephine's apartment, a comfortable and spacious room, with a fine bird's-eye view of Paris, was empty.

Fancying his mistress was at some neighbour's gossiping, he bawled: "Josephine! Come here!"

Heads appeared, looking anxiously out of rooms on the same floor.

"Where is Josephine?" Loupart cried.

Mme. Guinon came forward.

"I don't know," she replied, stammering. "She complained of pains in her stomach last evening, and I was told she's gone."

"Gone? Gone where?" stormed Loupart.

"Why, I don't know; it was Julie who told me."

A freckled face, half hidden by a matted shock of hair, appeared. Julie was not reticent like her mother. She explained in a hoarse, alcoholic voice:

"It's quite simple. When I came in last night about four I heard groans in Josephine's room. I went to see and found Josephine writhing in pain as if she had been — poisoned."

"What did you do then?"

"Oh, nothing," declared Julie. "I just trotted away again; it wasn't my business, but the Flirt came and meddled in it."

"The Flirt! Where is she?"

The Flirt, a faded, wrinkled woman of fifty, appeared from a doorway where she had been listening.

"Where is Josephine?" demanded Loupart.

"At Lâriboisière hospital, ward 22, since you want to know."

After a moment's amazement, Loupart broke out furiously:

"You sent off Josephine in the middle of the night! You took her to a hospital for a little indigestion! Without asking my consent! Why she's no more ill than I am!"

"Have to believe she is," replied the Flirt, "since the 'probes' have kept her."

Loupart turned and tramped downstairs swearing.

"She'll come out of that a damned sight quicker than she went in!"

A few moments later Loupart entered Father Korn's saloon. Having set forth his plans to that worthy, the latter proceeded to demolish them.

"You can't do anything to-day, so there's no use trying. You'll have to wait till to-morrow at midday, the proper visiting hour."

Loupart recognised the truth of the publican's assertion and, calling for writing paper, sat down and scrawled a letter to his mistress.

"Motor," he cried to the cripple who was still at Mother Toulouche's basket, "tumble along with this note to Lâriboisière; look sharp, and when you get back I'll stand you a glass."

As the cripple hurried away he was all but knocked down by a newsboy, running and shouting:

"Extra! Extra! Get *The Capital*. Extraordinary and mysterious crime of the Cité Frochot. Murder of a woman."

"Shall I get a copy?" asked the publican.

Loupart stalked out of the saloon without turning.

"Oh, I know all about that," he cried.

Father Korn stood rooted to the spot at Loupart's answer.

"What! He knows already!"

VI
THE LÂRIBOISIÈRE HOSPITAL

The clerk, who had admitted Juve, withdrew, and M. de Maufil, the amiable director, gave the police officer his most gracious smile.

"When I applied this morning at headquarters for an officer to be sent here, I scarcely expected to receive so celebrated a detective, upon a matter which is really very commonplace."

"Your letter to M. Havard mentioned a person I have been looking for with the greatest interest for the past two days. Loupart, alias 'The Square,'" replied Juve, "that is why I came myself. What is it about, sir?"

"Well, the day before yesterday, we took in at the instance of Doctor Patel, a patient suffering from acute gastric trouble. The woman gave us for identification the name of Josephine, no calling, residing in Paris, Rue de Goutte d'Or, in furnished rooms. Some hours after her admission to the hospital, she received a letter, brought by a messenger, which threw her into a violent state of terror. The nurse on duty sent for me, and I succeeded, after great difficulty, in quieting her; but she insisted most emphatically on leaving the hospital at once. The poor creature was in a high fever, and to grant her request would have been sending her to her death. At length she intrusted me with the letter which had excited her so. Here it is, kindly look it over."

Juve took the letter and read:

> "Am just back from the doss. You ain't there, and I don't want any more of these dodges. You are no more ill than I am. See here, you'll either leave the hospital and slope back to the house right off or to-morrow, Friday, at visiting time, as sure as my name's what it is, you'll get two bullets in your hide to teach you to hold your tongue."

Juve gave a grunt of satisfaction.

"You understand what is going on?" asked the director.

"Yes, but please go on with your story."

"Well, sir, you can guess that having read this letter, I easily got from the girl some information as to the writer. According to what she told me this Loupart is her lover, and he seems to have in a high degree that inconceivable pride which causes folks of his class, when they have sworn to kill some one, to carry out their threat, no matter what risk they may run themselves. The girl, Josephine, is convinced that to-morrow Loupart will come and kill her."

"You have told her that all precautions will be taken?"

"Of course. I pointed out to her that people do not come in here as they do into a bar; that being warned, I should have all the visitors watched who come here and asked to see her. I repeated to her that her lover probably wanted to frighten her, but that he could not do anything to injure her. I insisted that in the state she was in it was physically impossible for her to obey that wretch's bidding."

"And what was her answer to that?"

"Nothing. Her attack of alarm having subsided she seemed to fall into a condition of extreme prostration. I realised quite well that she regarded herself as condemned, that she had a far higher opinion of Loupart's daring than of my watchfulness, and, lastly, if she stayed it was because she realised it was out of the question for her, in her weak state, to go back to her home."

While the director was speaking, Juve had retained a smiling and satisfied expression, seeming but little affected by Josephine's terrible plight.

"I should very much like to know," continued the director, "why you said you knew the reasons for the threat being sent by this man to his mistress?"

Juve hesitated some moments; then, without going into details, said: "It would take too long to recount the motives which prompted Loupart to write that letter. This Josephine whom you see to-day trembling at her lover's threat not so long ago supplied the police with valuable hints concerning him. Has he learned that? Does he know the woman has rounded on him? Did he fear, above all, that she would tell tales again here at the hospital? It is quite possible. You see he must have had very strong reasons for giving her the order to come home —— ”

Juve here broke off, fingering Loupart's letter; then at length he placed it in his pocketbook.

“I will keep this document, director; it is a tangible proof of Loupart's criminal intentions. If he should put his threats into practice it would be difficult after that to deny premeditation.”

“You think that such a thing is possible?”

“Don't you?”

“Loupart declares he will come to the hospital before three and kill his mistress, but surely it must be easy to render that impossible.”

“You think the police are all-powerful, that we can arrest would-be murderers and render them incapable of harm? That is an error. We are prevented from taking effective action by a swarm of regulations. If I met Loupart on the street I would not be able to arrest him. I have no warrant. When a man holds his life cheap and is determined to risk everything, he has a pretty good chance of succeeding. Of course I shall take every measure to prevent Loupart killing his mistress, but I'm not at all sure of success.”

“But M. Juve, we must have this girl Josephine transferred to another hospital if necessary.”

Juve shook his head.

“And show Loupart we are aware of his purpose? Flatter the ruffian's vanity? No, we must let Loupart come, and catch him as he is about to commit the crime.”

“What do you propose to do?”

“Study the hospital; arrange where to place my men,” replied Juve.

“In that case, I will do everything I can to help you.” M. de Maufil rang for an attendant and bade him take Juve to Doctor Patel's department.

Juve thanked the obliging director and took leave. The attendant pointed to a row of windows under the roof.

“Doctor Patel's division begins at the corner window and runs to the window near the cornice.”

“What are the means of access to the female ward?”

“Oh, that's quite simple, sir; you get into the woman's ward either by the door on the staircase or by the door at the back, which leads into the laboratory of the head physician, the room of the house surgeon on duty, and the departmental offices.”

“And how do visitors pass in?”

“Visitors always go up the main staircase.”

“Now,” said Juve, “show me over Doctor Patel's division.”

“Very good, sir. It will be all the more interesting to you, as it is just the visiting hour.”

When Juve made his way into the woman's ward, Doctor Patel was actually in process of seeing his patients. He was passing from bed to bed, questioning each of the women under treatment and listening to the comments of the house staff who followed him.

“Gentlemen,” the doctor was saying as Juve joined the group, “the patient we have just seen affords a very excellent and typical instance of intermittent fever. The serum tests have not given any appreciable result; it is therefore impossible to arrive at —— ”

A hand was laid on Juve's shoulder.

“Why, the tests are always absolutely indicative! Palpable typhoid, eh? What do you think?”

Juve turned his head and could not suppress a cry of surprise.

“Doctor Chaleck!”

“What! M. Juve! — You here! Were you looking for me?”

Juve was dumbfounded. He drew Chaleck aside.

“Then you're attached to this hospital?”

“Oh, I have only leave to attend the courses.”

“And I came here out of curiosity.”

"In any case, allow me to thank you for the service you rendered me the other day. The officer who was with you seemed to take me for the guilty man."

"Well, you see, appearances...."

"But if anyone was a victim it was I. Apart from the finding of the murdered woman in my house, I have been robbed!"

Here the doctor broke off. A house surgeon was beckoning to him.

"Forgive me," he said to Juve. "I cannot keep my colleague waiting."

Leaving Chaleck, Juve went back to the attendant who had patiently waited for him.

"Stranger than ever!" he murmured. "There is no making it all out. Josephine writes that Loupart means to rob Chaleck. I track Loupart and he gives me the slip. I spend a night in a room where I see nothing, and where nevertheless a horrible amazing crime is committed. The murder takes place scarce a yard from me, and the doctor, the tenant of the house, sees nothing either, and does not even know the victim who is found next morning on his premises! Thereupon our informant, Josephine, goes into hospital; pain in the stomach, they say — hem! Poison, maybe? Then she gets a threatening letter from Loupart. And when I come to the hospital to protect her, whom do I meet but Doctor Chaleck!"

Juve, turning to the attendant who was escorting him, asked:

"You know the person I was speaking to just now?"

"Doctor Chaleck? Yes, sir."

"What is his business here?"

"He is a foreign doctor, I believe. I should fancy a Belgian. Anyhow, he is allowed by the authorities to follow the clinical courses and make researches in the laboratory."

VII
A REVOLVER SHOT

Doctor Patel's division presented an unusually animated appearance that afternoon. Not only were the patients allowed to receive visitors, but quite a number of strange doctors had spent the day going from bed to bed, note-books in hand, studying the patients and their temperature charts. The nurses hesitated to call these individuals doctors, and the patients, too, seemed aware of their true status. Whispers were hushed, and all eyes turned toward the far end of the ward.

There, in a bed set slightly apart and near the house staff's quarters, lay Josephine, a prey to a racking fever and breathing with difficulty.

Exactly opposite her was the bed of an old woman who had been admitted that morning. Her face had almost entirely disappeared under voluminous bandages.

As the ward clock struck a quarter to three, an attendant appeared and announced:

"In ten minutes visitors will be requested to leave."

Two of the staff who had paced the ward since early in the day exchanged a smile.

"Here's the end of the farce," remarked one; "Loupart isn't coming."

"He said three; there are still thirteen minutes left," replied the other.

"Well, every precaution is taken."

"Precautions are of no use with men like Loupart."

"Eleven minutes left."

"What the devil could happen? There is no longer admission to the hospital; the visitors are leaving."

"Three minutes!"

"Look here, you'll end by making me think..."

"Two minutes."

"Well, own yourself beaten!"

"One minute."

Bang! Bang! Two shots from a revolver suddenly startled the silent ward.

There was a moment's consternation and uproar. The patients leaped from their beds and sought refuge in the corners of the ward, while the two house surgeons and the policemen, passing as doctors, rushed in a body toward Josephine's bed. Doors slammed. People came hurrying from all quarters.

Above the hubbub rose a calm voice.

"What the devil! Here I am drenched! What does that mean?"

The house surgeon reached the bed where the hopeless Josephine lay, white as a corpse, motionless. A large red blood stain was spreading on her sheet. Quickly the doctor uncovered the wounded woman and examined her.

"Fainted, she has only fainted!" And, silencing all comments, he called:

"Monsieur Juve! Monsieur Juve!"

The old woman who, a few moments before, had been dozing, now quickly sprang out of bed, and, tearing off her bandages, revealed the placid features of detective Juve.

"I understand everything except that I'm drenched to the bones," declared Juve, as he crossed to Josephine's bed, oblivious to the amazement his appearance caused.

"That's easily explained," said the house surgeon. "The girl was lying on a rubber mattress filled with water. One of the bullets punctured it."

"What damage did she receive?"

"A contusion on the shoulder. The murderer aimed badly owing to her recumbent position."

Juve beckoned to the officers.

"Your report? You've seen nothing?"

"Nothing."

"That's strange," declared the detective. "I kept an eye on Josephine myself, thinking that a movement on her part would betray the entrance of Loupart. She made no sign; but, however Loupart may have got in, he can't get out without falling into a trap. I have fifty men posted round the building. Now, the first point to clear up is the exact place from where the shot was fired."

"How can we get at that?"

"Very simply. By drawing an imaginary line between the spot where the bullet struck the mattress and where it went into the floor — extend this line and we find the quarter from where the shot was fired." A doctor came forward.

"M. Juve," he said, "that would bring us to the door of the staff's room."

"Ah, it's you, Doctor Chaleck! I'm glad to see you! You are quite right in your surmise. Do you see any objection to my reasoning?"

"I do. I came into the ward barely two seconds before the firing. No one was behind me and no one was walking before me."

Juve crossed to the door.

"It is from here that the shots were fired!"

And the detective added triumphantly as he stooped and picked up an object from the floor: "And this backs up my assertion!"

He held out a revolver, still loaded in four chambers. "A precious bit of evidence!" He turned to the doctor:

"Can a stranger get into the wards by this door?"

"Utterly impossible, M. Juve! Only those thoroughly familiar with Lâriboisière can get into the ward through the laboratory. You must pass through the surgical divisions."

The detective seated himself at the foot of the sick woman's bed and mechanically laid the revolver beside him. But scarcely had he done so when he sprang up. Upon the sheet was a tiny red speck left by the muzzle of the weapon.

"Ah! — that's very instructive!" he cried. And as the others crowded round, puzzled, Juve added: "Don't you see? The murderer ran his finger along the barrel to steady his aim, and as the barrel is very short, the bullet grazed the tip of his finger which extended slightly beyond it. If I find anyone in the hospital with a wounded finger, I've got the murderer! Gentlemen, I am going to ask the director to issue orders for everyone within the hospital gates to pass before me. I reckon that in two hours at most the culprit will no longer be at large."

The attempted murder happened at three o'clock; about six o'clock, those who had first been examined by Juve had received permission to leave the hospital and were beginning to depart.

With a careless step Doctor Chaleck made for the exit by which he issued every evening from Lâriboisière. As he was about to pass out, a police inspector barred his way.

"Excuse me, sir. Have you a pass?"

"A pass?"

"Yes, sir; no one is allowed to leave to-day without a pass from M. Juve."

The doctor looked at his watch.

"The deuce," he said. "I'm late as it is. Where am I to get this pass?"

"You must ask M. Juve himself for it. He is in the director's private room."

"All right, I'll go there." And Doctor Chaleck retraced his steps.

VIII

THE SEARCH FOR THE CRIMINAL

"It's astounding!" declared M. de Maufil. "We have already examined nearly two hundred persons and found nothing."

"That may be," replied Juve, "but we may discover the culprit by the two hundred and first hand held out to us."

"There is one thing you forget, M. Juve."

"What is that?"

"If the culprit gets wind of our method of investigation, if he has any notion that you are inspecting the hands of all those who desire to leave the hospital, he won't be such a ninny as to come and submit to your inspection."

Juve nodded approval of the comment.

"You are right; but I have taken means to obviate that difficulty."

Since he had begun his inquiry on the spot, from the very moment when the revolver shots had rung out, the great detective was growing more and more sure that the arrest of the mysterious offender would be a matter of considerable time. The buildings of the establishment were extensive, and it was easy for a man to move about them without attracting attention. They offered really strange facilities for hiding.

"Mr. Director," said Juve, "I fancy we have inspected pretty well all the persons who leave Lâriboisière as a rule, at this time?"

"That is so."

"Then we must now change our plan. Let us leave a nurse here to detain those who come to ask for passes, and begin a search of the hospital ourselves. I shall post my officers in line, each man keeping in sight the one behind and the one before him. At the foot of every staircase I shall leave a sentry. Then, beginning at the outer wall of the building we will drive everyone on the ground floor toward the other end. If we don't round up our man there, we will proceed to the floor above."

"A good idea," replied M. de Maufil. "We shall catch him in a trap."

When Doctor Chaleck found that the inspector watching the exit leading to the main door in the Rue Ambroise Paré refused him leave to pass out of the hospital without the sanction of the great detective, he had perforce to retrace his steps. Skirting the bushes in the courtyard he took his way toward the medical wards, turning his back on the directoral offices, where he might have encountered our friend Juve. He had taken off his white uniform and was dressed in his street clothes. He halted at the entrance to the long glazed gallery which extends to the operating rooms of the surgical department. Turning suddenly, he saw in the distance and coming his way Inspector Juve, accompanied by the director. He noticed at the same time the cordon of officers preparing to sweep the hospital from end to end. Mechanically, and as if bent on putting a certain distance between him and the new-comers, he turned into the glazed gallery, and reached the far end of it. He was about to go into the surgical ward when a nurse stopped him.

"Doctor, you can't go in just now; Professor Hugard is operating and has given express orders that no one is to be admitted."

Chaleck turned up the gallery again, but abruptly swung round again as he caught sight of Juve and the director just entering the gallery, driving before them half a dozen patients and orderlies. Chaleck joined this little group, which had pulled up at the end of the gallery and was making laughing comments on the rigid inspection to which Juve was just about to subject them.

"Now's the time to show clean hands," joked a non-resident, "eh, Miss Victorine?" he added, smiling at a buxom nurse whom the chances of duty had blockaded in the corridor.

"Depend upon it," growled one of the accountants of the administrative department, shrugging his shoulders, "they are making a great fuss over nothing. After all, no one is hurt. Just one more pistol shot; in this neighbourhood we have ceased to count them."

An old man, who had his hand bandaged, suggested: "Perhaps they'll be wanting to arrest me since the culprit is wounded in the fingers, they say."

Dignified and calm, Juve did his best to restore liberty to each of the persons brought together. They had only to show their two hands held up in front of the face, the fingers apart. M. de Maufil, at a sign from Juve, immediately bade the attendant hand the person in question a card bearing his name and description. Armed with this "Sesame" he could come and go unimpeded all over the hospital.

Pointing to a large door at the extreme end of the corridor, Juve asked:

"What exit is that?"

The other smiled. "You want to see everything, don't you?"

The director, opening the heavy door, made room for Juve, who entered a very narrow passage, damp and quite dark. The passage, a short one, opened on a vast apartment, much like a cellar, lighted by air-holes in the ceiling and intensely cold. A noise of running water from open taps broke with its monotonous splash the silence of this place, solely furnished with a huge slab of wood running from one end to the other. Upon the slab dim and lengthy white shapes were outstretched, and when his eyes grew accustomed to the twilight, Juve recognised the vague outline of these weird bundles. They were corpses swathed in shrouds. The heads and shoulders alone were visible, and on the brows of the dead trickled icy water, dispensed sparingly but regularly by duck-billed taps that overhung the inclined plane.

The director explained: "This is the amphitheatre where we keep the bodies for post-mortems. Do you want to stay any longer?"

"There is no access to the room except by the door we came in at?"

"None."

"In that case," rejoined Juve, "and as there is no furniture here for a person to hide in, let us look elsewhere. It's a rather gruesome place."

"You're not used to the sight, that's all," replied the director, as he led the way back to his office.

Juve looked at his watch. "Well, I must leave you now and make a report to M. Havard. I'm afraid the murderer has slipped through our fingers."

"But you'll come back?"

"Of course."

"What am I to do meanwhile?"

"Nothing, unless you care to go over the hospital again."

"And the passes? Are they to be in force still? We have no one in the place but the staff."

"That is essential," replied Juve. "I must know with certainty who comes in and goes out. However, anyone known to your doorkeeper who wishes to leave need only sign in a register."

IX
IN THE REFRIGERATORY

It was light in the evening. One by one the rooms in Lâriboisière were being lit up.

The one exception was the grim amphitheatre, whose occupants would never need to see again.

Suddenly — and if anyone had been present, he would have experienced the most frightful impression it is possible to conceive — a corpse stirred.

Having assured himself that the door between the amphitheatre and the gallery was shut, the corpse, shivering with cold, threw off the shroud which enveloped him, and set to work to move his legs and arms about to start up his circulation. Then at the far end of the apartment this living corpse discovered, under a zinc basin attached to the wall, a bundle of linen and garments, which he seized upon.

His body shaking with cold, the man dressed himself in haste, and then waited until he considered his clothes sufficiently dry not to attract attention.

Carefully ascertaining that the gallery was deserted, he then entered it and walked rapidly to the courtyard. To the right of the main gateway, the smaller gate leading into the Rue Ambroise Paré was open.

The man passed under the archway, and in a moment would have been clear of Lâriboisière, when the doorkeeper barred his way.

"Excuse me, who goes there?"

Then, having looked more closely:

"Why it's Doctor Chaleck! You're late in leaving us this evening, doctor. I suppose you've been kept pretty busy in ward 22?"

"That's so," replied Chaleck, for it was he. "That's why I'm in a hurry, Charles."

And Chaleck, with an impatient gesture, was about to slip out, but the porter stopped him again.

"One moment, doctor; you must register first."

"Is this a new hospital regulation?"

"No, doctor, it's the police who have ordered everyone entering or leaving the hospital to sign his name in this book."

The porter, having taken Doctor Chaleck into his lodge, opened a new register, and pointing to half a dozen names already written on the first page, he added:

"You'll not be in bad company; you're to sign just below Professor Hugard."

Chaleck smiled. "Tell me the latest news, Charles. Do they suspect anyone?"

"All I know is that fifty of them came here with dirty shoes, made a hubbub round the patients, put the service out of gear, and in the end caught nobody at all. But if the culprit is still here, he won't get out without the bracelets on his wrists!"

An equivocal smile touched the pale lips of Chaleck. It might be the weird inhabitant of the little house in Cité Frochot was not so sure as the porter was of the astuteness of the police. Perhaps he was thinking that a few hours before a certain Doctor Chaleck, hemmed in a passage with no exits and about to be compelled to show, like everyone else, the tips of his fingers, had, under the nose of the officers, and even of the artful and astute Juve, suddenly vanished, gone out of the world of the living and thought it necessary, for reasons he alone knew, to assume the rigidity of a corpse, the stillness of death. But the smile in a moment became frozen.

The doctor who had kept both hands in his pockets while talking to the porter, suddenly felt a sharp twinge in the fingers of his right hand, and it became moist and lukewarm. This happened as the porter held out the register for him to sign.

"Charles," he cried, "I'm in a great hurry; while I'm signing, please go out and stop the first taxi that passes."

"Certainly, sir," replied the man.

Scarcely had the doorkeeper turned his back when the doctor, with infinite precautions drew out his right hand and with evident difficulty began to write, holding the pen between the third and fourth fingers, as though unable to use the fore and middle ones.

As he was finishing his entry, he made what was doubtless an unintended movement, something unexpected happened, for he suddenly turned pale and repressed a heavy oath. Charles was just coming back to the lodge.

"Your taxi is here, Doctor."

"Right. Thank you."

Chaleck closed the register abruptly, jumped into the motor, threw an address to the driver, who got under way. On seeing the doctor shut the register, Charles cried: "The devil — there's no blotting paper in it, it will be sure to blot!"

And, though it was too late, the careful man rushed to the book and opened it. His eyes became fixed on the page where the signatures were. He stared, wide-eyed.

"Oh! — Oh! — " he murmured.

X
THE BLOODY SIGNATURE

M. de Maufil was exceedingly nervous.

"As soon as you went back to headquarters," he declared to Juve, some moments after that officer had been shown into his private room, "I continued the search with redoubled efforts. Neither the ward-nurses, in whom I place complete confidence, nor the heads of my staff, whom I have known for ever so long, passed the doors of the hospital. In fact, I took every precaution and obeyed your instructions to the letter — yet all in vain."

"You found nothing?"

"Nothing. Not only did we not discover the criminal, but we did not come upon any trace of him."

"That's strange.".

"It is maddening. It would seem that from the instant the man fired those two shots in the woman's ward in Patel's department he vanished, unaccountably. Your notion of examining the hands of all those in the hospital was an excellent one, but nothing came of it.

"He must have known the snare we were preparing for him and did not turn up at the hospital exit, so we must naturally conclude he is still inside the gates, hidden in some remote corner, or underground. However, the first thing to do is to protect the girl, Josephine. By the by, she saw nothing, I suppose?"

"She declares she did not see Loupart come in, but she asserts with a sort of perverse pride that it was certainly Loupart who fired at her because he had threatened to do so."

A knock at the door was followed by the timid entrance of the doorkeeper.

"Is that you, Charles? Come in," cried the director. "What do you want?"

"It's about the signature, sir. There is blood on my book."

In a moment Juve leaped from his chair and tore the register out of the porter's hands. "Blood!"

Feverishly he turned the pages until he came to the writing. Without waiting for de Maufil's permission, he dismissed the porter.

"Very good, I'll see you presently."

Scarcely had the door shut, when Juve pointed to the page. "Look! Doctor Chaleck's signature! And just below it this mark of blood! What do you say to that, sir?"

"But it's sheer madness. Chaleck cannot be guilty!"

"Why not?"

"Because he is known to me. He was recommended to me seven months ago by an old comrade of mine. Chaleck is a man of brains, a foreign physician, a Belgian. He comes here specially to study intermittent fevers. M. Juve, I tell you he has nothing whatever to do with this affair." Juve picked up his hat and stick. He was restless and uneasy; the directors' outburst had not greatly impressed him.

"Doctor Chaleck could not explain how his finger came to be hurt and he did not inform us of the fact."

"A mere coincidence."

"Possibly, but it is a terrible coincidence for that man," replied Juve.

On leaving the director's room, the distinguished detective could not refrain from rubbing his hands. "This time I have him!" he muttered. He went rapidly down the stairs, crossed the great courtyard of the hospital, and proceeded to knock at the porter's lodge.

"Tell me, my friend, precisely how Doctor Chaleck's leaving the hospital came about?"

The worthy man with much detail, for he now felt very proud of having played a part in the affair, related how Doctor Chaleck came to the gate, sent him after a cab while signing his name, then made off, after having, no doubt by an oversight, closed the register.

"Very good! Thank you," was Juve's comment, bestowing a liberal tip on the man.

This time he was leaving Lâriboisière for good.

"Very characteristic, that piece of impudence," he reflected; "very like Doctor Chaleck that device of shutting the register he had just stained with blood in order to give himself time to make off!" On reaching the Boulevard Magenta he hailed a cab.

"Rue Montmartre. Stop at the *Capital* office. You know it?"

A few minutes later Juve was shown into Fandor's office. But the detective no longer wore a smiling face, and his air of abstraction did not escape his friend.

"Anything fresh?" inquired Fandor.

"Much that is fresh! That's why I came here to see you."

The journalist smiled. "Thanks, Juve. It is, indeed, owing to you that the *Capital* is the best posted sheet in town."

Then the detective proceeded to tell the reporter the startling discovery he had just made at Lâriboisière. He concluded:

"There, I suppose you can turn that into a thrilling story, eh?"

"I certainly can."

"The arrest is now scarcely more than a matter of time."

"And how are you going to set about it?"

"I don't quite know. Well, good-bye."

Fandor let the officer reach the door of the office, then called him back.

"Juve!"

"Fandor!"

"You are hiding something from me."

"I? Nonsense."

"Yes," persisted Fandor. "You are concealing something. Don't deny it. I know you too well, my friend, to be content with your reticences."

"My reticences?"

"You didn't come here merely to give me copy."

"Why —— "

"No. You had some idea in coming to look me up and then you changed your mind. Why?"

"I assure you you are mistaken."

Fandor rose.

"All right, if you won't tell me, I shall follow you." At the journalist's announcement Juve shrugged his shoulders.

"That's what I feared. But it's absurd to be always dragging you into risky affairs."

"Where are we going?" asked Fandor briefly, as he lit a cigarette.

"We are going to-night to Doctor Chaleck's. If he's there we will force a confession from him; if he's not there, we will ransack his house for clues," and Juve added, smiling, "like good burglars. I have a whole bunch of false keys. We shall be able to get into Doctor Chaleck's without ringing his bell. Here's a snapshot I took of Josephine at the hospital." And throwing the proof on Fandor's desk, he said smilingly:

"The young woman's not bad looking, is she?"

THE SHOWER OF SAND

"I'm afraid it's not quite the thing to enter people's houses in this fashion," whispered Juve, as the two men found themselves in the hall of Doctor Chaleck's little house in the Frochot district.

It was about midnight, and through the fan-light of the outer door a dim twilight enabled the detective and the journalist to get an idea of the place in which they stood.

It was a fairly large hall with double doors on either hand, leading into the drawing-and dining-rooms. At the far end rose a winding staircase, and under it a door to the cellar. A hanging lamp, unlit, was suspended from the ceiling and the walls were covered with dark tapestries.

Juve and Fandor remained silent and motionless for some moments. They might well be perturbed, for they had just entered the house in the most unwarrantable manner, and they knew the doctor to be at home. The lodge-keeper of the Cité had seen him return about two hours ago. For one moment Juve had asked himself whether he should not ring in the most natural manner in the world, and afterwards contrive some explanation; but the silence, the peace which prevailed and the conviction that Doctor Chaleck, quite off his guard, must be enjoying deep slumber, prompted him to try and get into the house unannounced. If the door was only bolted, if it was not secured from within by a latch, the officer might reckon on finding among his pass keys one that would allow him to open it. Juve was, indeed, equipped like the prince of burglars.

Well, the attempt had succeeded. Without trouble or noise, journalist and officer had made their way into the place.

Before imparting to Fandor his plan of operations, Juve handed him a pair of rubbers, and then at a signal they both ascended to the first floor.

The detective's plan was to make a sudden incursion into Chaleck's bedroom, and in the surprise of a sudden awakening, question him and inspect the fingers of his right hand, which, presumably, had left on the register a tell-tale trace of blood.

Juve had scarcely entered the room when Fandor switched on the lights; the two men started back in disgust; the room was empty!

Without pause, Juve cried: "To the study!"

A moment later they found themselves in the room they knew so well from having spent a whole night there, behind the window curtains.

Chaleck was not there either. Fandor searched the bathroom near by, careless of the noise he made, then hurried after Juve to the floor below in the fear that the doctor might already have made his escape.

Juve quickly reassured him the windows and shutters of the rooms were hermetically closed; the hall door had not been touched.

Suddenly slight sounds became audible from the floor above. A crackling of the boards, the muffled sounds of hasty footsteps, faint rustlings.

"Chaleck knows we are here," whispered Juve. "We must play with our cards on the table."

The two men cocked their pistols and made a rush upstairs. They had left the electric light burning on the floor above, and at first their eyes were dazzled by the sudden brightness, multiplied by the reflection from the glass which lined the octagonal-shaped landing.

Again the noises were heard. Chaleck or some one else was in the study.

Juve disappeared. In half a minute he returned and bumped into Fandor.

"Where are you coming from?" he cried. "I thought you were behind me."

"So I was," replied Fandor, "but I left you to take a look in the study."

"But it was I who was in the study!"

Fandor stared in amazement. "Are you losing your senses?"

"I've just come from there myself!"

"Well, we weren't there together, that's certain. Let's try again."

The two proceeded in the dark to the head of the staircase. With their heels they verified the last step; then Juve said in a low voice:

"I will go forward four paces. I am now in the middle of the landing; I lift the curtain, turn and go in."

The steady tick of the little Empire clock on the mantelpiece assured Juve that he was indeed in the study.

"Well, here I am," and mechanically he flung his hat on the sofa. But scarcely had he uttered these words when Fandor's voice, very clear, but some way off answered

"I am in the study, too."

Juve now switched on the light. Fandor was not there. Rushing back to the landing he ran full tilt into his friend and the two gripped each other in amazement.

"Look here," exclaimed Fandor, "if I'm not mistaken, you turned to the right past the curtain while I went to the left; there may be two separate entrances to the study."

"Let us keep together this time," replied Juve; "I propose to get to the bottom of this mystery."

As they came out of the darkness of the passage and plunged into the full light of the room, Juve stopped short. His hat was no longer on the sofa.

Fandor went to the mantelpiece, turned and confronted the detective.

"I stopped the clock some moments ago, and here it is going and keeping exact time! How do you account for it?"

Juve was about to reply, when suddenly with a dry click the light went out.

Fandor, at the same moment, gave a startled cry: "Juve! the door is fastened; we are shut in!"

With one bound Juve leaped for the window; but after opening the casement he perceived that thick iron shutters, padlocked, banished all hope of escape in that quarter. Fandor was ashy pale; Juve staggered as he moved toward him.

"Walled in!" he cried. "We are walled in!"

But a new terror suddenly confronted the two men. The floor appeared to be giving way, and as the descent proceeded regularly, they realised that they were in a strange form of elevator.

The study, however, did not drop very far. With a slight shock it reached the end of the run and stopped short.

Juve cried with an air of relief, "Well, here we are, and it now remains to find out where we are."

The existence of two studies identical in every particular, one of which was housed in an elevator, explained not only the events of the evening, but also the tragedy of two days before.

"Juve! did you feel anything?"

"Yes."

"What is it?"

"I don't know."

Both had just experienced a weird sensation, impossible to define. Upon their hands and faces slight prickings irritated the skin. The air at the same time seemed heavier and more difficult to breathe. There was, besides, a soft, vague crackling. With some difficulty Juve lighted his pocket-lamp. By its faint glimmer the two men made a discovery. A fine rain of sand was falling from the ceiling.

"It's collapsed!" cried Fandor.

"We're done for!" replied Juve.

They passed through some awful moments. All around the sand gathered and rose.

Juve tried to comfort his friend:

"It would need an enormous amount of sand to fill this room and bury us alive. It will cease to fall presently."

But horrible to relate, as the level of the sand rose on the floor, they observed by the flickering gleam of the lamp, that the ceiling was now being lowered little by little.

Fandor raised his arm and touched it. They were about to be crushed.

"Juve, do not let me die this way. Kill me!"

His comrade made no reply. At first paralysed by the shock he now felt an unspeakable fury rise up in him. He began beating the walls with his fists, shaking the furniture. He seized a chair and drove it against the door. The chair struck with a ring upon metal and broke.

Uttering a loud sigh, the detective drew out his revolver; he would, at least, save his friend the torments of an awful death. Suddenly a fearful crash resounded. The moving mass of sand was falling away from them into some gaping hole below, while at the same time fresh, moist air reached them and refreshed their lungs. Evidently some communication with the outside world had been established.

Juve relit his lamp and was bending over to examine what had taken place when the floor all at once gave way under his feet and he fell, dragging Fandor with him.

They found themselves up to mid-leg in water, but unhurt.

Juve's voice rang out: "We are saved! I see now what happened! Our trap had a thin flooring, and, when down, it rested on a fragile arch. That arch gave way, and with the sand we have tumbled into the sewer of the Place Pigalle, which, if I am not mistaken, connects with the main of the Chaussée d'Autin. Come along, friend Fandor, we'll find means to get out of this before long."

Floundering in the mud, they made their way along the drain until Juve halted and uttered a cry of triumph. On the left wall of the vault his hand encountered iron rings one above the other. It was a ladder leading to one of the manholes in the pavement. He quickly climbed up and, with a vigorous push, raised the heavy slab. In a few moments both men emerged and fell exhausted in the roadway.

When Fandor recovered his senses he was lying in a large, ill-lighted hall. The first sound he heard was Juve's voice arguing hotly and volubly.

"Why, you're nothing but a pack of idiots! We burglars! It's utter rot. I tell you I'm Juve, Inspector of Public Safety!"

XII

FOLLOWING JOSEPHINE

The captives had been recognised, and had been set at liberty. They had scarcely got a few yards from the police station, when Juve took the journalist's arm.

"Let's make haste!" he cried. "This foolish arrest has made us lose precious hours."

"You have a plan, Juve? What is it?"

"We must now turn our attention to Josephine; we must use her as a bait to catch the others. The girl won't be much longer at Lâriboisière. She will be extremely anxious to leave that place and — — "

"And go back to clear herself of treachery in Loupart's eyes? Is that it?" added Fandor.

"Exactly. Accordingly here is our plan of action. I must go at once to the Prefecture and advise M. Havard of our adventure. Meanwhile you go to the hospital. Contrive to see Josephine, make sure she has not left, watch her and then — wait for me; in two hours, at the latest, I shall be with you."

"All right, Juve, you can reckon on me. Josephine shall not escape me."

Fandor was already moving off when Juve called him back.

"Wait! If ever for one reason or another you want an appointment with me, telegraph to the Safety, room 44, in my name. I will see that the messages always reach me."

A quarter of an hour later Fandor was turning into the Rue Ambroise Paré, when all at once as he passed a woman he gave a start.

"Hullo!" he cried; "that's something we didn't bargain for!..."

The woman walked along the Boulevard Chapelle toward the Boulevard Barbès. Fandor followed her.

When the great clock which adorns the main front of the Lâriboisière buildings struck six, the nurses in the hospital were busy finishing their preparations for the night.

The surgeon in Dr. Patel's division was just concluding his evening visit to the patients. With a word of encouragement and cheer he passed from bed to bed until he reached the one at the end of the ward. The young woman occupying it was sitting up.

"So you want to be off," exclaimed the surgeon.

"Yes, doctor."

"Then you're not comfortable here?"

"Yes, doctor, but — — "

"But, what? Are you still afraid?"

"No, no."

The patient spoke these last words so confidently that the surgeon could not help smiling.

"Do you know," he observed, "that in your place I should be much less confident. What are you going to do? Where do you think of going when you leave here? Come, now, you are still very weak; you had much better spend the night here. You could go to-morrow morning after the round at eleven. It would be much more rational."

The young woman shook her head and replied curtly:

"I want to go now, sir, at once."

"Very good. They will give you your ticket."

The doctor gone, the young woman quickly jumped out of bed and began to dress herself.

"You don't suppose I'm going to stay here a minute longer than I have to," she grumbled with a laugh to her neighbour, who was watching her preparations with an envious eye.

"Some one waiting for you?"

"Sure there is. Loupart won't be pleased that I'm not back yet."

"Are you going from here to his place?"

"You bet I am."

This she said in a tone that showed plainly she found the thing quite natural. The other was not of her mind.

"Oh, well, I should be scared only at the thought of seeing that man. You were jolly lucky not to have been killed by him. And when he has got hold of you — — "

But Josephine laughed merrily.

"My dear," she said, "you don't know what you're saying. Depend on it, if Loupart didn't kill me it's because he didn't want to. He's a splendid shot. I suppose he had his reasons for not wanting me to stay here; I don't know his affairs, and besides, I came here without consulting him."

A vigorous "hush" from the nurse on duty stopped the conversation.

Josephine meanwhile completed her toilet. A nurse had brought her back the clothes she wore when she entered the hospital. She slipped on a poor muslin skirt, laced her bodice, buttoned her boots and set her curls straight; she was ready.

"I'm off," she cried gaily to the porter as she held out her pass to him. "Thank the Lord, I'm going, and I have no fancy to come back to your hotel!"

Once in the street, Josephine walked quickly. She cast a glance at the clock at a cabstand, and found she was behind time.

She went along the Rue Ambroise Paré, then turned on to the outer boulevards.

The dinner-hour being at hand, the populous streets of the Chapelle quarter were at their lowest ebb of animation. The bookshops had long since released their employees, the cafés were giving up their customers. Fandor, having recognised Josephine, followed her closely as she passed the outer boulevards, then by Boulevard Barbès.

"Beyond a doubt she is bound for the Goutte d'Or," he muttered.

Some minutes later, sure enough, she reached her home.

"Very good! The bird is back in the nest: My job is now to watch the visitors who come to call on her."

Opposite Josephine's door there was a wine-shop. This Fandor entered.

"Writing materials, please," he ordered. "I must drop a line to Juve," he thought. "We must begin to set the trap."

He was busy drawing up a detailed plan of the neighbourhood when, on raising his head, he gave a violent start, and, throwing a coin on the table, rushed out of the shop.

"She is well disguised, but there's no mistaking her!"

Without losing sight of the woman he was watching, Fandor reached the Metropolitan Station.

"Good Lord! What does this mean?" he muttered. "Where is she off to? She's taking a first-class ticket. Can she have an appointment with Chaleck?" He also took a ticket behind the young woman and reached the platform.

"I'm going where she goes," he thought. "But where the devil are we bound for?"

Loupart's mistress was the embodiment of a charming Parisian.

Her gown was tailor-made, of navy blue, plain but perfectly cut; she wore little shoes with high heels, and no one would have recognised in the well-dressed woman, who got out of the Metropolitan at the Lyons Station, the burnisher, who, a little while ago, had left Lâriboisière.

Josephine had scarcely taken a few steps on the great Square which divides Boulevard Diderot from the Lyons Station, when a young man, quietly dressed, came toward her. He ogled her, then in a voice of marked cordiality, said:

"Can I say a few words to you?"

"But, sir — — "

"Two words, mademoiselle, I beg of you."

"Speak," she said at last, after seeming to hesitate, halting on the edge of the pavement.

"Oh, not here; surely you will accept a glass?"

The young woman made up her mind:

"Very well, if you like."

The couple directed their steps toward a neighbouring "brasserie," and neither the young man nor Josephine dreamed of noticing that a passer-by entered the place in their wake.

Fandor did not take a seat at one of the little tables outside, but made for the interior, cleverly finding means to watch the two in a glass.

"Is this the person Josephine was to meet?" he wondered. "Can he be a messenger of Loupart's? Yet she did not seem to know him. Hullo!"

Just as the waiter was bringing two glasses of wine to the table where Josephine and her partner had seated themselves, the young woman suddenly arose, and, without taking leave, made for the door.

Fandor managed to pass close to the deserted man. He heard the waiter jokingly say:

"Not very kind, the little lady, eh?"

"I should think not! Didn't take her long to give me the slip."

Then in a tone of regret the young man added: "Pity, she was a nice little thing."

"That's all right," thought Fandor. "Now I know that Josephine accepted the drink because she thought he was sent by Loupart or one of the gang. Once enlightened as to his real object, she left him abruptly."

Tracking the young woman, Fandor now felt sure he was going to witness an interesting meeting. Josephine, however, seemed in no hurry. She inspected the illustrated papers in the kiosks, and presently reached the box where platform tickets are distributed; having taken one, she sat down near the foot of the staircase which leads to the refreshment rooms. Behind her Fandor also took a ticket, and, going up the stairs, leaned against the balustrade.

"I am waiting for some one," he said to the waiter who appeared. "You may bring me a cup of coffee."

Scarcely five minutes had passed, when Fandor saw a shabby looking man approach Josephine and begin an earnest conversation.

The man drew from his pocket a greasy note-book. From it he took a paper which he handed to the young woman, who promptly put it away in her handbag.

Fandor was puzzled.

"Where was she going? Why did this person hand her a ticket?"

The man pointed to a train where passengers were already taking their seats.

"The Marseilles train! So Loupart has left Paris!"

Then he called a messenger.

"Go and get me a first-class ticket to Marseilles. Here is money. Is there a telegraph office near at hand?"

"On the arrival platform, sir."

"Right. I will give you a message to take; go and hurry back."

Fandor took out his note-book and scrawled a message:

"Juve, Prefecture of Police, Room 44.

"Have met Josephine and followed her. She is off first class, by Marseilles train. Don't know her destination. Will wire you as soon as there's anything fresh.

"Fandor."

XIII

ROBBERY; AMERICAN FASHION

"Tickets, please."

The guard took the one offered by Fandor.

"Excuse me, sir, there's a mistake here," he said.

"This train doesn't go to Marseilles?"

"The train, yes, but not the last carriage in which you are, for it is bound for Pontarlier, and will be slipped at Lyons from this express."

Fandor was nonplussed. The essential was to follow Josephine, ensconced in the compartment next to his.

"Well, I'll get into another carriage when we are off; it's so easy with the corridors."

"You can't do that, sir," insisted the guard. "While all the carriages for Marseilles in the front of the train communicate, this one is separated from them by a baggage car."

"Then I'll change later, during the night. I have till Dijon, haven't I?"

"You have."

The guard went away. Fandor suddenly asked himself:

"Has Josephine made a mistake, too? Or has she a definite purpose in being in a carriage which is to be slipped from the Southern Express at Dijon to go on toward the Swiss frontier?"

The guard was looking at tickets in Josephine's compartment. Fandor went near to listen; he heard the tail of a conversation between the fair traveller, her companion and the guard. The latter declared as he withdrew:

"Exactly so, you shall not be disturbed."

When Josephine had boarded the train, Fandor had not ventured to watch her too closely, nor the companion she had met on the platform at the last moment. He now decided to take advantage of the corridor to take a look at the man.

He was quite stout, rather common in appearance, although with a prosperous air. A man of middle age, whose jolly face was framed in a beard, giving him the look of an old mariner. Moreover, he was one-eyed.

Josephine was playful, full of smiles and amiability, but also somewhat absent-minded.

The pair had decidedly the appearance of being lovers.

Although it was quite early, passengers were arranging to pass the night as comfortably as possible. The lamps had been shaded with their little blue curtains, and the portières, facing the corridors, had been drawn.

Fandor returned to his compartment. Two corners of it were already occupied — the two furthest away from the corridor. One was in possession of a man about forty, with a waxed moustache, having the air of an officer in mufti, the other was taken by a young collegian with a waxen complexion.

The journalist determined to keep awake, but scarcely had he settled himself when drowsiness crept over him. Rocked by the regular motion of the train he sank into a slumber troubled by nightmares. Then suddenly he sprang up. He had the clear impression of some one brushing by him and opening the door to the corridor.

"Who is there?" he murmured in a voice thick with sleep and drowned by the rush of the train. No one answered him. He staggered out into the corridor. At the far end of the carriage a passenger, with a long black beard, was standing smoking a cigar, and apparently studying the murky country. Not a sound came from Josephine's apartment. With a shrug of his shoulders and cursing his fears, Fandor returned to his own seat.

Why should he fancy, because he was following Josephine, that all the passengers in the train were cut-throats and accomplices of Loupart's mistress? Yet, five minutes after these sage reflections, Fandor started again; he had distinctly seen, passing along the corridor, two fellows with villainous faces and suspicious demeanour. One of them cast into Fandor's compartment such a murderous glance that it made the journalist's heart palpitate.

Fandor glanced at his companions. The officer was sleeping soundly, but the young fellow, although keeping perfectly still, opened his eyes from time to time and cast uneasy glances about him, then pretended to sleep as soon as he caught Fandor watching him.

The train slackened speed; they were entering Laroche Station; there was a stop to change engines. The officer suddenly awoke and got out. The compartment holding Josephine and her companion was thrown open, and, strange to say, his neighbour, the collegian, had moved into it, sitting just opposite the stout gentleman.

Fandor, with a view to keeping awake, abandoned his comfortable seat and settled himself in one of the hammocks in the corridor. He chose the one just opposite Josephine's door. But so great was his weariness that he quickly fell into a deep sleep. Suddenly a violent shock sent him rolling to the cross-seat in Josephine's compartment. As he picked himself up in a dazed condition, a cry of terror broke from his lips. Three inches from his head was the muzzle of a revolver held by a big ruffian wearing a mask, who cried:

"Hands up, all!"

Fandor and his companions were too amazed to immediately obey, and the command came again, more forcible.

"Hands up, and don't stir or I'll blow out your brains."

And now a gnome-like individual appeared, also masked.

The first one turned to Josephine: "You, woman, out of here!"

Without betraying by her expression whether or no she was his accomplice, Josephine hurriedly left her place and, slipping between the gnome and the colossus, went and cowered down at the end of the carriage.

"Go on!" suddenly commanded the big ruffian, who seemed to be the leader. "Go on! rifle 'em!"

The gnome, with wonderful adroitness, ransacked the coat and waistcoat pockets of the traveller. The stout man, shaking with alarm, made no resistance. After relieving him of his watch and pocketbook, they forced him to undo his shirt. Around his waist he wore a broad leather belt.

"Go it, Beaumôme, relieve him of his burden, the fat jackass!"

From the body of the traveller, the stolen belt passed to the big masked robber, who weighed the prize complacently. The belt contained pockets stuffed with gold and bank notes. The two robbers then moved away toward the further end of the carriage.

Fandor, furious at being tricked like the simplest of greenhorns, determined to seize the occasion to give the alarm.

The emergency bell was immediately above the pale-faced collegian. With a bound the journalist sprang for it, but fell back with a loud cry as he felt a sharp pain in his hand. The collegian had leaped up and cruelly bitten his finger. So great was the pain that Fandor swooned for a few seconds, and that gave his assailant time to cross the compartment and reach the corridor. At this moment the express slackened its speed and slowly came to a standstill.

"Is it too high to jump?"

Fandor knew the voice: it was Josephine's.

"No," answered some one. "Let yourself go. I'll catch you."

The sound of heavy shoes on the footboard told him that the robbers were making off. Josephine went with them, so she was their accomplice. The journalist sprang into the corridor to rush in pursuit. But he recoiled. A shot rang out, the glass fell broken before him, and a bullet flattened above his head in the woodwork.

It now seemed to him that the train was gradually gathering way again. Fandor put his head through the broken glass and searched the darkness outside.

"Ah!" he cried in amazement. There was no longer a train on the track, or rather, the main body of the train was vanishing in the distance, while the carriage in which he was and the rear baggage car had pulled up. Apparently the robbers had broken the couplings.

At the moment, the stout man, having quite recovered, drew near Fandor and observed the situation.

"Why, we're backing! We're backing!" he bellowed with alarm.

"Naturally, we're going down a slope," calmly replied Fandor. The other groaned and wrung his hands.

"It's appalling! The Simplon express is only twelve minutes behind us!"

Fandor now realized the frightful danger. Without delay he made for the carriage door, ready to jump and risk breaking his bones rather than face the terrible crash which seemed inevitable. But before he could make up his mind to the leap, a grinding noise became audible. The guard in the baggage car had applied the Westinghouse brakes and in a few minutes they came to a stop.

Fandor and the stout gentleman sprang frantically out of the carriage, and two brakemen jumped from the baggage car, crying: "Get away! Save yourselves!"

Clambering over the ties, they jumped a hedge, floundered in a hole full of water, scratching their hands and tearing their clothes; they rolled down a grassy slope, stuck in a ploughed field, then dropped to the ground, motionless, as a fearful din burst like thunder on the hush of the night. The Simplon express, racing at full speed, had crashed into the two carriages left on the rails and smashed them to bits, while the engine and forward carriages of the train were telescoped.

XIV
FLIGHT THROUGH THE NIGHT

Scarcely had Loupart received Josephine in his arms, as she jumped from the carriage, than he strenuously urged his companions to make haste.

"Now, then, boys, off we go, and quickly, too! Josephine, pick up your skirts and get a move on!"

It was a dark night, without moon, favourable to the robber's plans. For a good fifteen minutes the ill-omened crew continued their retreat by forced march. From time to time Loupart questioned the "Beard":

"This the way?"

The other nodded assent: "Keep on, we'll get there."

At length they descried the white ribbon of a road winding up the side of the low hill and vanishing in the distance into a small wood.

"There's the track," declared the Beard.

"To Dijon?"

"No, to Verrez."

"That's a good thing; now, stop and listen to me."

Loupart sat down on the grass and addressed them.

"It's been a good stroke, friends, but unfortunately it's not finished yet. They took precautions we couldn't foresee. We have only part of the fat. We share up to-morrow evening."

He was answered by growls of disappointment.

"I said to-morrow evening," he repeated. "Those who aren't satisfied with that can stay away. There'll be all the more for the others. Now, we must separate. Josephine, you, the Beard and I will get back together. There's work for us in Paris. The others scatter and take care not to get pinched; be back in the nest by ten."

Loupart motioned to the Beard and Josephine to follow him.

"Show us the way, Beard."

"Where to?"

"The telegraph office."

"What's up?"

"Why, you idiot," replied Loupart, "we've been robbed! The wine-dealer's notes are only halves! The swine insured himself for nothing."

The Beard broke out into recriminations.

"To have a hundred and fifty notes in your pocket, and they good for nothing! There was no such thing as Providence! It was sickening."

"Come, don't get angry, two halves will make a whole."

"You know where to lay hands on the rest?"

"Yes, old man."

"That's our job to-morrow evening? That's why you're chasing to the telegraph office?"

Loupart clenched his fists.

"That and something else; there's bigger game afoot."

"What?"

"Juve."

"Oh, the devil!" murmured the Beard, divided between pleasure and fear. "You've got the beggar?"

"I have."

"Sure?"

"Sure."

The little group moved forward in silence. At length Josephine began to tire.

"Say, have we much further to go?"

"No," replied the Beard. "Verrez village is behind that hill. The main road runs by the row of poplars."

"All right. Go and wait there with Josephine. I'll catch you up in a quarter of an hour," ordered Loupart. "I've a wire to send off."

His acolytes gone, Loupart resumed his way. As a measure of precaution, he took off his jacket, turned it inside out and put it on again. The jacket was a trick one: the lining was a different colour and the pockets differently placed.

On reaching Verrez, Loupart turned round. From the top of the little hill he could see, in the distance, the reddening flames.

"That's going all right," thought the wretch; "the Simplon express has run into the cars. There must be a fine mix-up there."

Reaching the post-office at last, he seized a blank and wrote on it hastily:

"Juve, Inspector of Safety, 142 Rue Bonaparte, Paris. All is well; found gang complete, including Loupart. Robbery committed but failed. Cannot give details. Be at Bercy Stores alone, but armed, to-morrow at eleven at night, near the Kessler House cellars.

"Fandor."

The clerk held out her hand to take the message. The bandit was extremely polite.

"Be so good as to pay special attention to this message. Read it over, madam. You grasp the importance of it? You see it must be kept absolutely secret. I rely on you."

Ten minutes' quick walking brought Loupart once more to Josephine and the Beard.

"Hullo!" he cried. "Anything new?"

"Nothing."

"Josephine, go down the hill and the first motor that passes, set to and howl; call 'help' and 'murder'; got to stop it. Be off! Look sharp!"

Some minutes passed. The two men watched Josephine go down the road and hide in one of the ditches.

"Your barker is ready, Beard?"

"Six plugs, Loupart."

"Good! You go to the right, I to the left."

Loupart had scarcely given these orders, when, on the horizon, a bright gleam became visible, growing larger every minute, while the noise of a motor broke the silence of the open country.

Loupart laughed.

"Look, Beard. Acetylene lamps, eh? That car will do our job splendidly."

An automobile was fast nearing them. As it passed by Josephine, she rushed into the road, uttering piercing cries.

"Help! Murder! Have pity! Stop!"

With a hasty movement the chauffeur, taken aback by the sight of a woman rising unexpectedly on the lonely road, made a dash at his brakes. Meanwhile from the inside of the car a traveller leaned out.

"What is it? What's the matter?"

As the car was about to stop, Loupart and the Beard rushed out.

"You take the passenger!" cried the former; "I'll attend to the chauffeur."

The two brigands sprang on the footboards.

"No tricks, or I'll shoot! Josephine, truss these fowls for me!" cried Loupart.

Josephine took a roll of cord from her lover's pocket and tied the two victims firmly while Loupart gagged them.

"Now, Beard, take them into the field and give them a rap on the head to keep them quiet."

Then he got into the car and skilfully turned it round. When Josephine and the Beard were on board, he got under way at full speed with a grim smile.

"And, now, Juve, it's between us two!"

XV

THE SIMPLON EXPRESS DISASTER

While Loupart and his mates were making off across country the disaster occurred. At a curve in the track the Simplon Express coming at full speed charged the cars and crushed them, then, lifted by the shock, the engine reared backwards on its wheels and fell heavily, dragging down in its fall a baggage car and the first two carriages coupled behind it. Then rose in the night cries of terror and the frantic rush of the passengers who fled from the luxurious train.

Fandor picked himself up and went forward. From the tender of the engine a cloud of steam escaped with hoarse whistlings.

The driver held out his two broken arms.

"Give me a hand, for God's sake! Open the tap! There, that hoisted bar. Lift it up. Quick, the boiler is going to burst."

Fandor was still engaged in carrying out this manoeuvre when succour began to arrive.

The stoker, less seriously hurt than the driver, had managed to drag himself clear of the wreckage, which was beginning to catch fire. The head guard, and those passengers whose seats had been at the rear of the train, hurried up and the combined effort at rescue began. They searched for the injured and put out the incipient blazes.

Instinctively those who had fled from the train followed in a frantic stampede the road at the foot of the embankment, reached Verrez village out of breath and gave the alarm.

The countryside was soon in an uproar. Lights flashed, torches and lamps of vehicles harnessed in haste: a quarter of an hour after the disaster half the neighbourhood was afoot from all quarters.

"A bit of luck, sir," remarked the conductor, still pallid with horror, to Fandor, "that the collision happened at the curve where our speed was slackened. Ten minutes sooner and all the carriages would have been telescoped."

"Yes, it was luck," replied the journalist, as he wiped his face, covered with soot and coal dust. "The two carriages telescoped were almost empty."

From a neighbouring way-station the railway officials had telephoned news of the accident. The section of line was kept clear by telegraph. Word came that a relief train was being made up, and would arrive in an hour.

Fandor had quickly regained his coolness, and was one of the first to lend a hand in the rescue, turning over the wreckage and setting free the injured.

As he passed along the track, he was attracted by the appeals of a stout man, who hurried toward him, wailing:

"Sir! Sir! What a terrible calamity!"

Fandor recognised his fellow-passenger, Josephine's lover.

"Yes, and we had a lucky escape. But what has become of your wife?"

In using the word "wife" Fandor was under no illusion; he merely wanted to interview the other.

"My wife? Ah, sir, that's the terrible part of it. She's not my wife — she's a little friend, and now it's all bound to come out. My lawful wife will hear everything. As for the girl, I don't know what has become of her."

"She knew that you were carrying money?"

"Yes, sir. I am an agent for wines at Bercy, and I was going to pay over dividends to stockholders, one hundred and fifty thousand francs. I recognised one of my men among the robbers, a cooper. He knew that every month I travel, carrying large sums of money. I am quite sure this robbery was planned beforehand."

"And who are you, sir?"

"M. Martialle, of Kessler & Barriès. Fortunately the money is not lost."

"Not lost! You know where to find the robbers?"

"That I do not, but they have only the halves of the notes. These are worth nothing to them unless they can lay their hands on the corresponding halves. It's a way of cheap insurance."

"And where are the other halves of the notes?"

"Oh, in a safe place, in the office of the firm at Bercy."

Fandor abruptly left M. Martialle and approached an official.

"When will the line be cleared?"

"In an hour's time, sire."

"There'll be no train for Paris till then?"

"No, sir."

Fandor moved off along the track.

"That's all right, I can make it. I'll have time to send a wire to *The Capital*."

The journalist sat down on the grass, took out his writing-pad and began his article. But he had overrated his strength. He was worn out, body and soul. He had not been writing ten minutes when he dropped into a doze, the pencil slipped from his fingers and he was fast asleep.

When Fandor opened his eyes, the twilight was beginning to come down. It was between five and six o'clock.

"What a fool I've been! I've made a mess of the whole business now," he cried as he ran frantically to the nearest station.

"How soon the first train to Paris?"

"In two minutes, sir: it is signalled."

"When does it arrive?"

"At ten o'clock."

Fandor threw up his hands.

"I shall be too late. I haven't time to wire Juve and warn him. Oh! what an idiot I was to sleep like that!"

XVI
A DRAMA AT THE BERCY WAREHOUSE

Juve passed the whole day at the Cité Frochot. Despite the precautions taken to keep the failure two days back a secret, the papers had got wind of the drama: *The Capital* itself had spoken of it, though without naming his fellow-worker. The staff of that paper was unaware that Fandor was the other man who had so marvellously escaped from the sewer. Blood-curdling tales were told about Doctor Chaleck, Juve, Loupart, the house of the crime, the affair at the hospital; but to anyone familiar with the actual happenings, the newspaper accounts were very far from giving the truth.

And Juve, far from contradicting these misstatements, took a delight in spreading them broadcast.

It is sometimes useful to set astray the powerful voice of the Press so as to give a false security to the real culprits.

However, when masons, electricians and zinc-workers were seen to take possession of Doctor Chaleck's house and begin to turn it upside down, a crowd quickly assembled to witness the performance.

It was with great difficulty that Juve, who did not want too many witnesses round the place, organised arrangements of a vigorous character.

Installed in the drawing-room on the ground floor, he first had a long interview with the owner of the house, M. Nathan, the well-known diamond broker of the Rue de Provence. The poor man was in despair to think his property had been the scene of the extraordinary events which were on everybody's tongue. All he knew of Doctor Chaleck was that that gentleman had been his tenant just four years, and had always paid his rent regularly.

"You didn't suspect," asked Juve in conclusion, "the ingenious contrivance of that electric lift in which the doctor placed a study identically similar to the real one?"

"Certainly not, sir," replied the worthy man. "Eighteen months ago my tenant asked permission to repair the house at his own expense; as you may suppose, I granted his request at once. It must have been at that time that the queer contrivance was built. Have I your permission to go down to the cellars and ascertain their condition?"

"Not before to-morrow, sir, when I shall have finished my inspection," replied Juve, as he saw M. Nathan out.

The inspector was assisted in his investigation by detectives Michel and Dupation. They interviewed the old couple in charge of the Cité and various neighbours of Doctor Chaleck, but without lighting upon a clue. Nobody had seen or heard anything whatever.

Toward noon he and Michel, who did not wish to leave the house, decided to have a modest repast brought to them. M. Dupation, a fidgety official, took this chance of getting away.

"Well, gentlemen," he declared, "you are much more up to this business than I, and besides my wife expects me to luncheon. You don't need any further help from me?"

Juve reassured the worthy superintendent and gave him permission to go. He was only too glad to find himself alone with his lieutenant. The workmen who were repairing the caved-in basement of the little house were already gone, and there was no chance of their being back before two o'clock. Thus Juve found himself alone with Michel.

"What I can't understand, sir," said Michel, "is the telephone call we got toward morning from here asking for help at the office in the Rue Rochefoucauld. Either the victim herself 'phoned, and in that case she did not die, as we think, in the early part of the night, or it was not she, and then —— "

Juve smiled.

"You are right in putting the problem that way, but to my mind it is easy to solve. The call was not given by the murdered woman for, remember, when we raised the body at half-past six it was already cold. Now the call was not given till six, when the woman had been dead some little time. That I am sure of, and you will see the report of the medical expert will uphold me."

"Then it was a third person who gave it?"

"Yes, and one who sought to have the crime discovered as soon as possible, and who reckoned on the officers coming from the Central Station, but did not expect Fandor or me to come back."

"Then according to you, sir, the murderer knew of your presence behind the curtain in the study while the crime was being committed."

"I can't tell about the murderer, but Doctor Chaleck certainly knew we were there. That man must have watched us all night, known the exact instant we left the house, and immediately afterwards got some one to telephone or must have done so himself."

Michel, becoming more and more convinced by Juve's reasoning, went on:

"At any rate, the existence of two studies, in all respects similar, goes to show a carefully premeditated plan, but there is something I can't account for. When you came back to the study where we found the dead woman, you found traces of mud by the window brought in by your shoes. You must therefore have been watching through the night the room where the crime was committed."

Juve was about to put in a word, but Michel, launched on his train of argument, continued:

"Allow me, sir; you are going, no doubt, to tell me that they might during your short absence have carried the body of the victim into the study in question, but I would point out to you, that on the loosened hair of the poor creature blood had caked, that some was on the carpet and had even gone through it to the flooring beneath. Now if they carried in the body just a little while before we discovered it, that would not have been the case."

Michel was delighted with his own argument. Juve smiled indulgently.

"My poor Michel," he cried, "you would be quite right if I put forward such an explanation. It is certain that the room in which we found the body was that in which the crime took place. It is therefore that in which we were not! As for the marks of mud near the window, they are ours, but transferred from the room in which we were into the room in which we were not! Which again proves that our presence was known to the culprits.

"Furthermore, the candle with which Doctor Chaleck melted the wax to seal his letters was scarcely used, it only burned in fact a few minutes. Now we found another candle in the same state. So you see that the precautions were well taken and everything possible done to lead us astray.

"We see the puppets moving — Loupart, Chaleck, Josephine, others maybe, but we do not see the strings."

"The strings which move them perhaps may be no other than — Fantômas," ventured Michel.

Juve frowned and suddenly fell silent. Then abruptly changing the conversation, he asked his lieutenant:

"You told me, did you not, that you could no longer appear in the character of the Sapper?"

"Quite true, Inspector, I was spotted just the day before the crime by Loupart, and so was my colleague, Nonet."

"Talking of that," answered Juve, "Nonet mentioned vaguely something about an affair at the docks, supposed to have been planned by the Beard and an individual known as the Cooper. Are you fully informed?"

"Unfortunately no, Inspector. I know no more about the matter than you do."

"And what is Nonet about now?"

"He has left for Chartres."

Juve shrugged his shoulders. He was annoyed. Perhaps if Léon, nicknamed Nonet, had not been transferred he would by now have obtained pertinent clues to the dock's affair.

After having enjoined Michel to devise a new disguise which allowed him to mix once more with the Band of Cyphers and going back to "The Good Comrades," Juve went down to the basement to supervise the workmen, who were now back; while Michel busied himself with the inventory of the papers found in Doctor Chaleck's study.

On leaving the house toward half-past seven in the evening Juve went slowly down to the Rue des Martyrs, pondering over the occurrences which for several days had succeeded each other with such startling rapidity.

As he reached the boulevards the bawling of newsboys attracted his attention. An ominous headline was displayed in the papers the crowd was struggling for.

"ANOTHER RAILROAD ACCIDENT.
THE SIMPLON EXPRESS TELESCOPES
THE MARSEILLES LIMITED. MANY
VICTIMS."

Juve anxiously bought a paper and scanned the list of the injured, fearful that Fandor would be found among the number. But as he read the details and learned that those in the detached carriage had escaped, he felt somewhat relieved. Hailing a taxi he drove off rapidly to the Prefecture in search of more precise information.

"A message for you, M. Juve."

The detective, hurrying home, was passing the porter's lodge. He pulled up short.

"For me?"

"Yes — it's certainly your name on the telegram."

Juve took the blue envelope with distrust and uneasiness. He had given his home address to no one. He glanced over the message, and gave a sigh of relief.

"The dear fellow," he muttered as he went upstairs. "He's had a narrow escape; however, all's well than ends well."

After a hurried toilet and a bite of dinner, Juve set off again, jumped into a train for the Boulevard St. Germain and got down at the Jardin des Plantes. Then, sauntering casually along, he made for Bercy by the docks, which were covered as far as the eye could see with rows and rows of barrels.

About two hours later, Juve, who had been wandering about the vast labyrinth of wine-docks, began to grow impatient.

It was already fifty minutes past the appointed hour, and the detective began to feel uneasy. Why was Fandor so late? Something must surely have happened to him! And then what a queer idea to choose such a meeting place!

Suddenly, Juve started. He recalled his talk that afternoon with Michel; the reference made to the affair of the docks in which the Beard and the Cooper were implicated. What if he had been drawn into a trap!

The detective's reflections were suddenly cut short by unusual and alarming sounds.

He fancied he heard the shrill blast of a whistle, followed by the rush of footsteps and a collision of empty barrels.

Juve held his breath and crouched down under the shed in which he stood; he thought he saw the outline of a shadow passing slowly in the distance. Juve was stealthily following in its tracks when he caught a significant click.

"Two can play at that," he growled between his teeth, as he cocked his revolver. The shadow disappeared, but the footsteps went on.

Disguising his voice he called out: "Who goes there?"

A sharp summons answered him, "Halt!"

Juve was about to call upon his mysterious neighbour to do likewise, when a report rang out, at once followed by another. Juve saw where the shots came from. His assailant was scarcely fifteen paces from him, but luckily the shots had gone wide.

"Use up your cartridges, my friend," muttered Juve; "when your get to number six, it will be my turn."

The sixth shot rang out. This was the signal for Juve to spring forward. Leaping over the barrels, he made for the shadow which he espied at intervals. All at once he gave a cry of triumph. He was face to face with a man.

His cry, however, changed into amazement.

"You, Fandor?"

"Juve!"

"You've begun shooting at me, now, have you?"

For answer, the journalist held out his revolver, which was fully loaded.

"But what are you doing here, Juve?" he asked.

"You wired to me to come."

"That I never did."

Juve drew the telegram from his pocket and held it out to Fandor, but as the two men drew close together, they were startled by a lightning flash, and a report. A bullet whistled past their ears. Instinctively they lay flat between two barrels, holding their breaths.

Juve whispered instructions: "When I give the signal, fire at anything you see or toward the direction of the next report."

The two men slowly and noiselessly raised their heads.

"Ah," cried Juve.

And he fired at the rapidly fleeing figure.

"Did you see?" whispered Fandor, clutching Juve's arm. "It's Chaleck."

Juve was about to leap up and start in pursuit when a series of dull thuds, the overturning of barrels, stifled oaths and cracking planks smote his ear. These noises were followed by the measured footfall of a body of men drawing near, words of command and shrill whistles.

"What's all that now?" questioned Fandor.

"The best thing that could happen for us," replied Juve. "The police are coming. These quays are a refuge for all kinds of tramps and crooks who from time to time are rounded up. We are probably going to see a 'drive.'"

Juve had scarcely finished speaking when several shots rang out; these were followed by a general uproar and then a great blue flame suddenly rose, died away and flared up again. A thick smoke permeated the atmosphere.

"Fire," exclaimed Fandor.

"The kegs of alcohol are alight," added Juve.

The two had now to think of their own safety. Evidently bandits had been tracking them for more than an hour, guided by Doctor Chaleck.

But they soon found that their retreat was cut off by a ring of flames.

"Let us head for the Seine," suggested Fandor, who had discovered a break in the ring of fire at that point. A fresh explosion now took place. From a burst cask a spurt of liquid fire shot up, closing the circle. It had become impossible to pass through in any direction.

They heard the cries of the rabble, the whistles of the officers. In the distance the horns of the fire engines moaned dolefully. The heat was growing unbearable, and the ring enclosing Fandor and Juve narrowed more and more. Suddenly Juve pointed to an enormous empty puncheon that had just rolled beside them.

"Have you ever looped the loop?" he asked. "Hurry up now; in you go; we'll let it roll down the slope of the quay into the river."

In a few moments the cask was rolling at top speed. Juve and Fandor guessed by the crackling of the outer planks and by a sudden rise in the temperature that they were passing through the fire. All at once the great vat reached the level of the river. It plunged into the waves with a dull thud.

XVII
ON THE SLABS OF THE MORGUE

As he turned at the far side of the Pont St. Louis, Doctor Ardel, the celebrated medical jurist, caught sight of M. Fuselier, the magistrate, chatting with Inspector Juve in front of the Morgue.

"I am behind-hand, gentlemen. So sorry to have made you wait."

M. Fuselier and Juve crossed the tiny court and entered the semi-circular lecture-room, where daily lessons in medical jurisprudence are given to the students and the head men of the detective police force.

Doctor Ardel, piloting his guests, did the honours.

"The place is not exactly gay; in fact, it has an ill reputation; but anyhow, gentlemen, it is at your disposition. M. Fuselier, you will be able to investigate in peace: M. Juve, you will be at liberty to put any questions you choose to your client."

The doctor spoke in a loud voice, emphasising each word with a jolly laugh, good natured, devoid of malice, yet making an unpleasant impression on his two visitors less at home than he in the gruesome abode they had just entered.

"You will excuse me," he went on, "if I leave you for a couple of minutes to put on an overall and my rubber gloves?"

The doctor gone, the two instinctively felt a vague need to talk to counteract the doleful atmosphere the Morgue seemed to exhale, where so many unclaimed corpses, so much human flotsam, had come to sleep under the inquiring eyes of the crowd, before being given to the common ditch, being no more than an entry in a register and a date: "Body found so and so, buried so and so."

"Tell me, my dear Juve," asked M. Fuselier. "This morning directly I got your message I at once acceded to your wish and asked Ardel to have us both here this afternoon, but I hardly understand your object. What have you come here for?"

Juve, with both hands in his pockets, was walking up and down before the dissecting table. At the Magistrate's question he stopped short, and, turning to M. Fuselier, replied:

"Why have I come here? I scarcely know myself. It's everything or nothing. The key to the puzzle. I tell you, M. Fuselier, things are becoming increasingly tragic and baffling."

"How's that?"

"The part played by Josephine is less and less clear. She is Loupart's mistress; she informs against him, is fired at by him, then, according to Fandor, becomes in some manner his accomplice in a robbery so daring that you must search the annals of American criminality to find its like."

"You refer to the train affair?"

"Yes. Now, leaving Josephine on one side, we are confronted with two enigmas. Doctor Chaleck, a man of the world, a scholar, crops up as leader of a band of criminals. What we know for certain about him is that he fired at Josephine, that he was concerned in the affair of the docks — no more. There remains Loupart; and about him being the real culprit we know nothing. There is no proof that he killed the woman. In order to prove that we should have to know who that woman is and why she was killed, and also how. The how and why of the crime alone might chance to give us the answer."

"What trail are you following?"

"That of the dead woman. The body we are about to examine will determine me in which quarter to direct my search."

M. Fuselier, looking at the detective with a penetrating eye, asked:

"You surely haven't the notion of suspecting Fantômas?"

"You are right, M. Fuselier," he replied. "Behind Loupart, behind Chaleck, everywhere and always it is Fantômas I am looking for."

Whatever information the detective was about to impart to the magistrate was cut short by the return of Doctor Ardel. That gentleman, in donning the uniform of the expert, had resumed an appearance of professional gravity.

"We are going to work now, gentlemen," he announced. "I need not remind you, of course, that the body you are about to see, that of the woman found in the Cité Frochot, has already undergone certain changes due to decomposition, which have modified its aspect."

So saying, Dr. Ardel pressed a button and gave an attendant the necessary order. "Be so good as to bring the body from room No. 6."

Some minutes later a folding door in the wall opened and two men pushed a truck into the middle of the hall upon which lay the corpse of the unknown.

"I now give over the dead woman to you to identify," declared Doctor Ardel. "My examination has been carried out and my part as expert is over — I am ready to hand in my report."

Fuselier and Juve bent long over the slab upon which the body had been placed.

"Alas!" cried Juve, "how recognise anything in this countenance destroyed by pitch? What discover in these crushed limbs, this human form, which is now a shapeless mass?" And, turning to Dr. Ardel, he questioned:

"Professor, what did you learn from your autopsy?"

"Nothing, or very little," replied the doctor. "Death was not due to one blow more than another. A general effusion of blood took place everywhere at once."

"Everywhere at once? What do you mean by that?" questioned Juve.

"Gentlemen, that is the exact truth. In dissecting this body I was surprised to find all the blood vessels burst, the heart, the veins, the arteries, even the lung cells. More than this, the very bones are broken, splintered into a vast number of little pieces. Lastly, both on the limbs and over the whole body I find a general ecchymosis, reaching from the top of the neck to the lower extremities."

"But," objected Juve, who feared the professor might linger over technical details too complex for him, "what general notion does this suggest to you as to the cause of death?"

"A strange idea, M. Juve, and one it is not easy for me to define. You might say that the body of this woman had passed under the grinders of a roller! The body is 'rolled,' that is just the word, crushed all over, and there is no point where the pressure might be conjectured to have been greatest."

M. Fuselier looked at Juve.

"What can we deduce from that?" he asked.

"Professor Ardel demonstrates scientifically the same doubts to which a rough inspection led me. How did the murderer go to work? It becomes more and more of a mystery."

"It is so much so," declared Professor Ardel, "that even by postulating the worst complications I really cannot conceive of any machine capable of thus crushing a human being."

"I do not believe," declared the magistrate, "that we have any more to see here. It is plain, Juve, that this corpse cannot furnish any clues to you and me for the inquest."

"The corpse, no," cried Juve, "but there is something else."

Then, turning to the professor, he asked:

"Could you have brought to us the clothes this woman wore?"

"Quite easily."

From a bag that an attendant handed him Juve drew out the garments of the dead woman. The shoes were by a good maker, the silk stockings with open-work embroidery, the chemise and the drawers were of fine linen and the corset was well cut.

"Nothing," he cried, "not a mark on this linen nor even the name of the shop where it was bought."

He examined her petticoat, her bodice, a sort of elegant blouse, trimmed with lace, and the velvet collar which had several spots of blood upon it. He then drew a small penknife from his pocket and, kneeling on the floor, proceeded to probe the seams. Suddenly he uttered a muffled exclamation:

"Ah! What's this?" From the lining of the bodice he drew out a thin roll of paper, crumpled, stained with blood, torn unfortunately.

> "Goodness of God in whom I trust — I do not wish to die with this remorse — I do not wish to risk his killing me to destroy this secret — I write this confession, I will tell him it is deposited in a safe place — yes, I was the cause of the death of that hapless actor! Yes, Valgrand paid for the crime which Gurn committed.... Yes, I sent Valgrand to the scaffold by making him pass for Gurn — Gurn who killed Lord Beltham, Gurn, who I sometimes think must be Fantômas!"

Juve read these lines in an agitated voice, and as he came to the signature he turned pale and was obliged to stop.

"What is the matter?"

"It is signed — 'Lady Beltham.'"

In order that Doctor Ardel, understanding nothing of Juve's agitation, might grasp that import of the paper just discovered he would have had to call to mind the appalling tragedy which three years before had stirred the whole world with its bloody vicissitude and mystery, one not solved to that hour.

"Lady Beltham!"

At that name Juve called up the whole blood-curdling past! He saw in fancy the English lady whose husband was murdered by the Canadian Gurn, who perhaps was her lover.

And Juve, following his train of thought, pondered that he had accused this same lady of having, to save her lover, the very day the guillotine was erected on the boulevard, found means to send in his stead the innocent actor, Valgrand.

And here in connection with this affair of the Cité Frochot he found Lady Beltham involved in the puzzle of which he was so keenly seeking the key.

Juve again read the momentous paper he had just unearthed.

"By Jove, it was plain," ran his thought, "the lady, criminal though she might be, was first and foremost Fantômas' passionate inamorata. And this paper he held in his hands was the tail end of her confession — the remains of a document in which in a fit of moral distress she had avowed her remorse and made known the truth."

And taking line by line the cryptic statement, Juve asked himself further:

"What do these phrases signify? How extract the whole truth from these few words? 'I do not want him to kill me in order to destroy that secret'! When Lady Beltham wrote that she was angry with Gurn. Then again what did this other doubtful expression mean? — 'Gurn who I sometimes fancy may be Fantômas.' She did not know then the precise identity of her lover! Oh, the wretch! To what depths had she sunk?"

Then as he put this query to himself, Juve shook from head to foot. Like a thunderclap he thought he grasped the truth he had followed so eagerly. What had become of Lady Beltham? Must he not come to the conclusion that this woman whose face had been crushed out of all recognition by the murderer was none other than the lady? How else explain the discovery in her bodice of the betraying document? Who but she could have had it in her possession? Who else could have so sedulously concealed it?

Juve read over another clause: "I will tell him it is deposited in a safe place."

Feverishly Juve took up the garments trailing on the ground, carefully explored the fabric, made a minute search.

"It is impossible," he thought, "that I should not find another document. The beginning of this confession — I must have it!"

All at once he stopped short in his search. "Curse it all!" And he pointed out to M. Fuselier, disguised in the lining of a loose pocket in the petticoat — a fresh hiding place, but torn and alas! empty.

This woman had split up her confession into several portions. And if she was killed it was certainly to strip her of these compromising papers. Well, the murderer had attained his object.

"Look, Fuselier, this empty 'cache' is the proof of what I put forward, and chance alone allowed the page concealed in the collar of this bodice to fall into my hands."

Long did the detective still grope and ponder, heedless of the questions the professor and the magistrate kept asking him. He rose at last, and with a distracted gesture took the arm of M. Fuselier, and dragged him before the stone slab on which the corpse, but recently unknown, smiled a ghastly smile.

"M. Fuselier, the dead woman has spoken. She is Lady Beltham. This is the body of Lady Beltham!"

The magistrate recoiled in horror. He murmured:

"But who then can Doctor Chaleck be? Who can Loupart be?"

Juve replied without hesitation.

"Ask Fantômas the names of his accomplices!"

And leaving him and Doctor Ardel without any farewell Juve rushed from the Morgue, his features so distorted that as they passed him people drew aside, amazed and murmuring:

"A madman or a murderer!"

XVIII
FANTÔMAS' VICTIM

"You understand my object, Fandor? Hitherto I have worked unaided. I wanted to unearth Fantômas and bring him to Headquarters, saying to my superiors, 'For three years you have maintained this man was dead; well, here he is! I have put the darbies on the most terrible ruffian of modern times.' Well, I must forego my little triumph. We must now work in the open. Public opinion must come to our aid."

"Then you want me to write my article?"

"Yes, and tell all the details; wind up by putting the question squarely. 'Is not Fantômas still alive?' Then sum up in the affirmative. Now, be off. I want to read your article this evening in the *Capital*."

Fandor had just left his detective friend when old Jean, the only servant that Juve tolerated in his private quarters, entered the room.

"Don't forget the person who is waiting in the parlour, sir."

"Ah, yes, to be sure. A person who comes to see me at home, when nobody knows my address should be interesting. Show him in, Jean."

Juve placed his revolver in reach of his hand as Jean announced: "Maître Gérin, notary."

Juve rose, motioned his visitor to a chair and inquired the object of his visit.

Maître Gérin bowed respectfully to Juve.

"I must apologise," he said, "for coming to disturb you at home, sir, but it concerns a matter of such importance and it involves names so terrible that I could not utter them within the walls of the Sûreté. What brings me here is a crime which must be laid to Fantômas or his heirs in crime."

Juve was strangely moved.

"Speak, sir, I am all attention."

"M. Juve, I believe that one of my clients, a woman, has been killed. I have had for some time a certain sympathy, and, I don't disguise it, an immense curiosity concerning her because she was actually involved in the mysterious affairs of Fantômas."

"The name of the woman, counsel, her name, I beg of you?"

"The name of the woman who, I fear, has been murdered is — Lady Beltham!"

Juve gave a sigh of relief. It was the name he wished to hear.

Maître Gérin continued: "I have been Lady Beltham's lawyer for a long period of time, but since the Fantômas case came to an end in the sentencing to death of Gurn and the subsequent scandal attached to the name of Lady Beltham, I have ceased to have any further tidings of that unhappy woman.

"Indirectly, through the medium of the papers which at times gave out some echo of her, I knew that she had been travelling, then, that she was back in Paris, and had gone to live at Neuilly, Boulevard Inkermann. But I did not see her again. It is true her family matters were settled, her husband's estate entirely wound up. In short, she had no reason to appeal to me professionally."

"To be sure."

"Well, some days ago, I was greatly surprised by her visiting my office. Naturally I refrained from asking her any awkward questions."

Juve interrupted: "In Heaven's name, sir, how long ago is it since Lady Beltham called on you?"

"Nineteen days, sir."

A sigh of relief escaped Juve. He had feared all his theories regarding the body at the Morgue the day before were going to collapse. "Go on, sir," he cried.

"Lady Beltham, on being shown into my private office, appeared to me much the same physically as I had known her previously, but she was no longer the great lady, cold, haughty, a trifle disdainful. She seemed crushed under a terrible load, a prey to awful mental torture. She made appeal to my discretion, both professionally and as a man of honour.

"She then spoke as follows: 'I am going to write a letter which, if it fell into the hands of a third person, would bring about a great calamity. This letter I shall intrust to you together with my Will which will instruct you what to do with it at my death. I will send you a visiting card with a line in my own handwriting every fortnight. If ever this card fails to come, conclude that I am dead, that they have murdered me, and carry that letter where I tell you — Avenge me!'"

"Well, what then?" cried Juve, anxiously.

"That is all, M. Juve. I have not seen Lady Beltham again, nor had any news of her. When I called at her residence I was told she was away. I have come to ask you whether you think she has been murdered."

Juve was pacing his room with great strides.

"Maître," he said at last, "your story confirms all I have suspected. Yes, Lady Beltham is dead. She has been murdered. That letter contained her confession and revealed not only her own crimes, but those of her accomplices, of her master — of — Fantômas. Fantômas killed her to free himself of a witness to his evil life."

"Fantômas! But Fantômas is dead."

"So they say."

"Have you proofs of his existence?"

"I am looking for them."

"What do you think of doing?"

"I am going to make an investigation. I am going to learn where and how Lady Beltham was killed. I shall see you again, Maître. Read *The Capital* this evening. You will find in it many interesting surprises."

XIX

THE ENGLISHWOMAN OF BOULEVARD INKERMANN

"To sum up what I have just learned."

Juve was seated at his desk, and those who knew the private life of the great detective would assuredly have guessed that he was gravely preoccupied. He was trying to extract some useful information from the notary's visit, some hints essential to the investigation he had taken in hand, and that at all hazards he meant to pursue to a successful termination. The task was fraught with difficulties and even peril. But the triumph would be great if he should succeed in putting the "bracelets" on the "genius of crime," as he had called him to his friend Fandor.

"Lady Beltham had gone to visit Gérin. She was an astute woman after all, and knew how to get her own way. There must have been powerful motives which urged her to write that confession. What were those motives?"

"Remorse? No. A woman who loves has no remorse. Fear? Probably, but fear of what?"

Juve, without being aware of it, had just written on the paper of his note-book the ill-omened name which haunted him.

"Fantômas!"

"Why, of course, Fantômas killed Lady Beltham, and killed her in the house of Doctor Chaleck, an accomplice. And Loupart, a third accomplice, got his mistress to write to me, and I believed the denunciation. Loupart got us to dog him, led me unawares behind the curtains in the study, and made me witness that Chaleck was innocent. Oh, the ruse was a clever one. Josephine herself, by the two shots she received some days later at Lâriboisière, became a victim. In short, the scent was crossed and broken."

The detective snatched up his hat, saw carefully to the charges of his pocket revolver, then gravely and solemnly cried:

"It is you and I now, Fantômas!" with which he left his rooms.

Juve and Fandor were entering a taxi-cab.

"To Neuilly Church," cried Juve to the driver. "And, now, my dear Fandor, you must be thinking me crazy, as less than two hours ago I sent you off to write an article, and here I come taking you from your paper and carrying you away in this headlong fashion. But just listen to the tale of this morning's doings."

Juve then gave a full account of Maître Gérin's visit and wound up by saying: "It is through Lady Beltham that we must unearth that monster, Fantômas."

"That's all very well," replied Fandor, "but as the lady is dead, how are we going to set about it?"

"By reconstructing the last hours of her life. We are now on our way to Lady Beltham's residence, Boulevard Inkermann."

"And what are we to do when we arrive there?"

"I shall examine the house, which is probably empty, and you are to 'pump' the neighbours, to ask questions of the tradespeople. I should attract too much attention if I were to do this myself, and that is why I dragged you away from your work."

Some moments later the taxi pulled up at the corner of Boulevard Inkermann.

"The house is number — " said Juve as he took Fandor by the arm. "Bless me, you remember the house! It is the one in which I arrested Gurn three years ago; that famous day he came to see Lady Beltham, disguised as a beggar."

The two friends soon found themselves at their destination. Through the garden railing, which was wholly covered with a dense growth of ivy, the two saw the house, which now looked very dilapidated.

"It doesn't look as if it had been inhabited for a long while," said Fandor.

"That's what we want to make sure of. Go and make your inquiries."

Fandor left his companion and made his way back to the commercial section of Neuilly. He stopped opposite a sign which read:

"Gardening done."

"Anyone there?" he inquired.

An old woman, standing in the doorway, came forward. "What can I do for you, sir?"

"If I am not mistaken, it was you who attended to Lady Beltham's garden?"

"Yes, sir, we kept her garden in order. But my husband hasn't worked there for several months, as Lady Beltham has been away."

"I heard she was coming back to Paris, and called to-day, but found the house closed up."

"Oh, I am sorry. Lady Beltham's an excellent customer and Mme. Raymond also bought flowers of us."

"Mme. Raymond. She is a friend of Lady Beltham?"

"Her companion. It is now close to a year that Mme. Raymond has been living with her. Oh! a very pleasant lady; a pretty brunette, very elegant and not at all proud."

Fandor thought it well not to seem astonished.

"Oh, yes, of course," he cried, "Mme. Raymond. I remember now. Lady Beltham's life is so sad and lonely."

"True enough," the woman replied, and, lowering her voice: "And then, what with all these tales of noises and ghosts, the house can't be too pleasant to live in, eh?"

Fandor pretended to be well posted. "People still talk of these incidents?"

"Oh, yes, sir."

Fandor did not venture to press the subject, and, taking leave of the worthy woman, he made his way back to the Boulevard. As soon as Juve caught sight of him in the distance he ran up eagerly.

"Well?"

"Well, Juve, what have you found out during my absence?"

"In the first place that it is exactly sixty-four days since Lady Beltham left Neuilly. I discovered this by the dates on a lot of circulars in the letter box. I also had a talk with a butcher's man and learned that Lady Beltham had a companion."

"Oh! I was bringing you that same news!"

"This Mme. Raymond is young, dark, very pretty. Can't you guess who she is?"

Fandor stared at Juve.

"You mean —— "

"Josephine. It's perfectly clear. We know Lady Beltham wrote a confession, that Fantômas suspected this and murdered her to get hold of it, and further that in this murder Loupart was involved. Josephine was introduced to Lady Beltham by Fantômas. A spy going there to betray the great lady and possibly entice her later to the Cité Frochot. Let us make haste, lad. We thought we had to follow the trail of Loupart and Chaleck, but we mustn't lose sight of Josephine. She may be the means of helping us to the truth."

XX
THE ARREST OF JOSEPHINE

The somewhat grim faces of Mme. Guinon, Julie and the Flirt lit up suddenly. Bonzille, the tramp set free by the police the day after the "drive" in the Rue Charbonnière, had opened the bottle of vermouth, and Josephine bustled around to find glasses to put on the table.

Josephine had visitors in her little lodging. There was to be a quiet lunch. On the sideboard attractive dishes were ready, a fine savour of cooking onions came from the dark corner in which Loupart's pretty mistress was doing hasty cookery over the gas.

"Neat or with water?" asked Bonzille, performing his office of cup bearer with comical dignity.

Mme. Guinon asked for plenty of water. Julie shrugged her shoulders indifferently; she didn't care so long as there was drink, while the Flirt, in her cracked voice, breathed in the loafer's ear: "How about a sip of brandy to put with it?"

The appetiser loosened tongues: they began to cackle. From a drawer Josephine got out a pack of cards, which the Flirt promptly seized, while Julie, leaning familiarly on her shoulder, counselled her:

"Cut with the left and watch what you are doing; we shall see if there's any luck for us in the pack."

Josephine had now been back three days from her painful journey and had not seen Loupart. The latter, after having abandoned the motor in some waste ground among the fortifications, had vanished with the Beard, only bidding his mistress go home as if nothing had happened and wait for news of him.

The Simplon Express affair had made a great stir in the fashionable world, and had produced considerable uneasiness among the criminal class.

To be sure no name had been mentioned, and apparently the police were not following any definite clue. Still, in the Chapelle quarter, and especially in the den of the "Goutte d'Or" and the Rue de Chartres, it was noticed that the absence of the chief members of the Band of Cyphers coincided with the date of the tragedy.

At first there had been some slight stand-offishness shown to Josephine on her return. She was greeted with doubtful allusions, equivocal compliments, with a touch of coldness, and folks were also amazed at not seeing Loupart reappear with her.

Josephine told herself that she must at all costs disabuse her neighbours of this bad impression, and that is why she had decided to give a luncheon party to her most intimate friends. These might also be her most formidable opponents, for such damsels as the Flirt and Julie, even big Ernestine, could not fail to be jealous of the mistress of a distinguished leader; besides, she was the prettiest woman in the quarter.

Joining the conversation from time to time, Josephine smiled and regained confidence. Her manoeuvre bade fair to be crowned with success.

As they sat down to table the door opened and Mother Toulouche came in, carrying a capacious basket.

"Well," cried the old fence, "I got wind that something was going on here, and I said to myself, 'Why shouldn't Mother Toulouche be in it as well?' One more or less don't matter, eh, Josephine?"

Josephine assented and made room for her. Before sitting down the old woman put her basket on the floor.

"If I invite myself, Fifine, I bring something to the feast. Here are some portugals and two dozen snails which will help out."

All at once, Josephine, who, despite the general gaiety, was absent-minded and preoccupied, rose and ran to the door, answering a knock. She was at bottom horribly uneasy at hearing nothing of her lover. She began to fear that the police for once might have got the upper hand. It was little Paulot, the porter's son, who rushed in quite out of breath.

"Mme. Josephine, mother told me to come up and warn you that two gentlemen were asking for you in the lodge just now. Two gentlemen in special 'rig.'"

"Do you know them, Paulot?"

"I don't, Mme. Josephine."

"What did they want of me?"

"They didn't say."

"What did your mother answer?"

"Don't know. Believe she told 'em you were in your den."

The occurrence cast a chill over the company. Little Paulot was given a big glass of claret, and when he had left the Flirt observed gravely:

"It's the cops."

"Why should they come and inquire for me?"

Julie tried to console her.

"Anyhow they'll not come up to your place."

Josephine was greatly upset. Were they after her or Loupart? Why had they withdrawn? Would they come back?

In a flash she burst out, beating her fist on the table:

"Bah! I've had enough of this, not knowing what is going to happen from one moment to the next. Sooner than stay here, I'll go and find out."

The Flirt suggested, with a spiteful smile.

"Go ahead, my girl, they won't be far away; go and ask them what they want."

"Very well," cried Josephine, "I will."

And the young girl emptied her glass to give her courage.

"And if you don't come back, we'll set your room to rights," cried the Flirt after her. "Good luck, try and not sleep in the jug."

Josephine rushed downstairs, and then, after a moment's hesitation, turned and went down the Rue de Chartres.

At first she noticed nothing unusual or suspicious. The faces of those she met were mostly familiar to her. But suddenly her heart stopped beating. Two men accosted her simultaneously, one on her right, the other on her left.

Her neighbour on the right asked very softly:

"Are you Josephine Ramot?"

"Yes."

"You must come with us."

"Yes," said Josephine, resigned.

A few moments later, Josephine, seated in a cab between the two men, was crossing Paris. The detectives had given the address: "Boulevard du Palais."

Loupart's mistress, taken on her arrival to the ante-room adjoining the private rooms of the examining magistrates, had not much time for reflection.

To be sure, she was not guilty. Not guilty? Well, at bottom the affair of the Marseilles train made Josephine uneasy. And the story of the motor, too, the motor taken by force from unknown travellers. What knowledge had the police of these events? When questioned, was she to confess or deny?

A little old man, bald and fussy, appeared at the end of the passage and called her.

"Josephine Ramot, the private room of Justice Fuselier."

Mechanically she went forward between her two captors, who pushed her into a well-lit apartment, in the corner of which stood a big desk. A well-dressed gentleman was sitting there, writing; opposite him, in the shadow, some one stood motionless. The magistrate raised his head; his face was cold and contained, but not spiteful.

"What is your name?"

"Josephine Ramot."

"Where were you born?"

"Rue de Belleville."

"What is your age?"

"Twenty-two."

"You live by prostitution?"

Josephine coloured and, with an angry voice, cried:

"No, your honour, I have a calling. I am a polisher."

"Are you working now?"

Josephine felt awkward.

"Well, to say the truth, at the moment I have no work, but they know me at M. Monthier's, Rue de Malte; it was there I was apprenticed, and —— "

"And since you became the mistress of the ruffian Loupart, known as 'The Square,' you have ceased to practise an honest calling?"

"I won't deny being Loupart's mistress, but as for prostitution —— "

The man Josephine had noticed standing in the shadow came forward and murmured a few words in the magistrate's ear.

"M. Juve," cried Josephine, moving toward the inspector with her hand out. She stopped short as the detective motioned to her that such a familiarity was not allowable, and the examination was resumed.

The magistrate, after having by some curt questions brought to light the salient points of Josephine's life, and clearly mapped out the speedy development of the honest little work girl into a ruffian's mistress, and in all probability, accomplice, began the interrogation on the main point.

At some length he narrated without losing a single change of her countenance, the various incidents of the evening begun in the railway which ended with the disaster to the Simplon Express.

Fuselier made Josephine pass again through her headlong exit from Lâriboisière, her quick passage through Paris when she was barely convalescent, and still suffering from the effects of the fever, her departure in the Marseilles Express, where she picked up half a score of footpads headed by her redoubtable lover; then the waiting in the silence of the night, the affray, the threats, and lastly, after breaking the couplings to the train, the dangerous flight of the band, the headlong rush through the country.

The magistrate wound up:

"You came to town afterwards, Josephine Ramot, in company with Loupart, called 'The Square,' and his factotum, the ruffian 'Beard.'"

Josephine, embarrassed by the steady glance of the magistrate, endeavoured to keep her face devoid of expression, but as in his recital the points of the adventure she had shared grew more definite, she felt she was constantly changing colour and at certain moments her eyelids quivered over her downcast eyes.

Evidently he was well posted. That young man who got into the same compartment as M. Martialle must certainly have belonged to the police. But for that the judge would never have known precisely what took place. Decidedly this was a bad beginning.

Josephine now dreaded to see the door open and Loupart appear, the bracelets on his wrists, followed by the Beard, similarly fettered, for beyond a doubt the two men had been nabbed.

Hunched up, her nerves tense, Josephine kept her mind fixed on one point. She was waiting anxiously for the first chance to protest. At a certain juncture the magistrate declared:

"You three, Loupart, 'The Beard' and yourself, shared between you the proceeds of the robberies committed."

As soon as she could get a word in, Josephine shouted her innocence.

Oh, as to that, no! She had not touched a cent from the business. She did not even know what was involved.

The exact truth was this. She was ill in the hospital when all of a sudden she remembered that Loupart had some days before bidden her be at all costs at the Lyons Station, on a certain

Saturday evening at exactly seven o'clock. Now that particular Saturday was the day after the attempt on her life. As she was much better she set off in obedience to her lover. She knew no more; she had done no more; she would not have them accuse her of any more.

The young woman had gradually grown warm, her voice rose and vibrated. The judge let her have her say, and when she had finished there was a silence.

M. Fuselier slowly dipped a pen in the ink, and in his level voice declared, casting a glance in Juve's direction:

"After all, what seems clearly established is complicity."

Josephine gave a start — she knew the terrible significance of the term. Complicity meant joint guilt.

But Juve intervened:

"Excuse me, in place of 'complicity' perhaps we had better say 'compulsion.'"

"I don't follow you, Juve."

"We must bear in mind, your honour, that this girl is to be pardoned to a certain extent for having obeyed her lover's order, more particularly at a time when the latter had gained quite a victory over the police. For in spite of the protection of our people, his attempt against her partially succeeded."

Taken aback, M. Fuselier looked from the detective to the young woman whom he regarded as guilty. Juve's outburst seemed to him out of place.

"Your pardon, Juve, but your reasoning seems to me somewhat specious; however, I will not press this charge against the girl; we have something better."

Turning to Loupart's mistress, the judge asked abruptly:

"What has become of Lady Beltham?"

Josephine was amazed by the question. She turned inquiring eyes toward Juve, who quickly said:

"M. Fuselier, this is not the moment — —"

The magistrate, dropping this line, again tackled Josephine on her relations with Loupart.

In a flash Josephine made up her mind. She would simulate innocence at all costs. With the craft of a consummate actress, she began in a low voice, which gradually rose and became impressive, insinuating:

"How pitiful it is to think that everyone bears a grudge against a poor girl who, some day in springtime, has given herself the pleasure of a lover! Is there any harm in giving oneself to the man who loves you? Who forbids it? No one but the priests, and they have been kicked out of doors!"

The magistrate could not help smiling, and Juve showed signs of amusement.

"But I am honest, and when I understand something of what was going on, I wrote to M. Juve. And what thanks did I get? Two bullet holes in my skin!"

M. Fuselier hesitated about turning his summons into a committal.

XXI
AT THE MONTMARTRE FÊTE

The fête of Montmartre was at its height. In the Place Blanche a joyous crowd was pressing round a booth of huge dimensions, splendidly lighted. On the stage a cheap Jack, decked out in many-coloured frippery, was delivering his patter:

"Walk in, ladies and gentlemen; it's only ten cents, and you won't regret your money! The management of the theatre will present to you, without delay, the prettiest woman in the world and also the fattest, who weighs a trifle over 600 pounds and possibly more; as no scale has yet been found strong enough to weigh her without breaking into a thousand pieces.

"You will also have the rare and weird sight of a black from Abyssinia whose splendid ebony hide has been tattooed in white. Furthermore, a young girl of scarcely fourteen summers will astound you by entering the cage of the ferocious beasts, whose terrible roarings reach you here! The programme is most interesting, and after these incomparable attractions, you will applaud the cinema in colours — the last exploit of modern science — showing the recent tour of the President of the Republic, and himself in person delivering his speech to an audience as numerous as it is select. You will also see, reproduced in the most stirring and life-like manner, all the details of the mysterious murder which at this moment engages public interest and keeps the police on tenter-hooks. The crime at the Cité Frochot, with the murdered woman, the Empire clock, and the extinguished candle: all the accessories in full, including the collapse of the elevator into the sewer. The show is beginning! It has begun!"

Among the throng surrounding the mountebank three persons seemed especially amused by the peroration. They were two gentlemen, very elegant and distinguished, in evening clothes, and with them a pretty woman wearing a loose silk mantle over her low dress.

She put her lips to the ear of the older of her companions, who, with his turned-up moustache and grey hair, looked like a cavalry officer.

She murmured to him these strange words:

"Squint at the guy on the left, the one passing before the clock-seller's booth. That's one of the gang. He was in the Simplon affair."

The pretty Parisian, so smartly dressed, was no other than Josephine. The young man with the fair beard was Fandor and the cavalry officer was Juve. The three now "worked" together. The partnership dated from the afternoon that Josephine escaped arrest, thanks to the lucky intervention of Juve.

The latter had little belief in the young woman's innocence, but by getting her on his side, he hoped to secure information as to Loupart's doings.

Juve was talking to a ragged Arab selling nougat to the passers-by.

"Ay, sir," explained the Arab. "I have been dogging little Mimile since two this afternoon."

"Bravo, my dear Michel, your disguise is a perfect success."

Josephine came suddenly close and pulled Juve by the sleeve, and then pointed to a group of persons who were crossing the Place Blanche. Without troubling further about the Arab, Juve at once began to follow this group, motioning to Josephine and Fandor to follow him closely. The three threaded their way through the crowd with a thousand precautions, seeking to avoid attention, yet not losing sight of their quarry. All three had recognised Loupart!

The outlaw, dressed in a long blouse, with a tall cap, and armed with a stout cudgel, was walking among half a dozen individuals similarly attired. By their garb they would be taken for cattle-herders from La Villette.

This group proceeded slowly in the direction of Place Pigalle, and Juve, who was pressing hard on his quarry, slackened his pace in order to let them forge ahead a little. The square, which was surrounded by brilliantly illuminated restaurants, was a flood of light, and the detective did not want people to notice him. Moreover, the pseudo-cattle-drivers had stopped, too: gathering round Loupart they listened attentively to his remarks, made in a low tone. Clearly they were accomplices of the robber, who, perhaps, realised that they were being followed.

Fandor, who had put his arm through Josephine's, felt the young woman's heart beating as though it would burst. They were all playing for high stakes. Josephine, especially, was in a compromising and dangerous plight. Not only had she to fear the wrath of her lover, but she ran the risk of being "spotted" by one of the many satellites of the gang of Cyphers, in which case her condemnation would be certain.

Fandor encouraged her with a few kind words:

"You know, mademoiselle, you mustn't be frightened. If I am not greatly mistaken, Loupart is about to be nabbed, and once in Juve's hands he won't get out of them in a hurry."

Josephine's perturbation was scarcely quieter, and Fandor, a trifle skeptical, asked himself whether in reality the girl was on their side or if she were not playing the game of false information. Suddenly something fresh happened.

Loupart, separating himself from his companions, entered a restaurant upon which the words

"The Crocodile"

were inscribed in dazzling letters on its front. The Crocodile comprised, like most night resorts, a large saloon on the ground floor and a dining-room on the first floor which was reached by a little stairway and guarded by a giant clad in magnificent livery. Above this were apartments and private rooms.

Just then, as it was near midnight, a number of carriages were bringing couples in evening dress, who mounted the staircase. To their great surprise, Fandor and Josephine saw Loupart make for this staircase. The long smock of the seeming cattle-driver would certainly make a queer showing. What was the formidable robber's game? Juve gave hasty directions:

"It's all right. I know the house. It has only one exit. You, Ramot," he went on, addressing the young woman, "go up to the first floor and take your place at a table; here are ten dollars, order champagne and don't be too stiff with the company."

Josephine nodded and went upstairs.

Juve and Fandor followed a few minutes later and took up a strategic position at a table near the doorway. Fandor had a view of the room and Juve commanded the hall and stairway. From the room came a confused hum of laughter, cries and doubtful jokes. A negro, clad in red and armed with a gong, capered among the tables, dancing and singing.

Fandor caught sight of Josephine, who appeared to be carrying out Juve's instructions. Beside her was a fair giant of red complexion and clean-shaven face, whose Anglo-Saxon origin was beyond doubt. Fandor knew the face; he had seen the man somewhere; he remembered his square shoulders and bull-like neck, and the enormous biceps which stood out under the cloth of his sleeves.

"By Jove!" he cried suddenly. "Why it's Dixon, the American heavyweight champion!"

Juve signalled to the waiter to bring him the bill as he fitted a monocle into his right eye. Fandor stared at him, surprised.

"Well, Juve, when you get yourself up as a man of the world, you omit no detail."

Juve made no reply for some moments, then turned to his companion.

"Who else do you see in the room?"

Fandor looked carefully, and then made a gesture of amazement.

"Chaleck! Chaleck is over there eating his supper!"

"Yes," said Juve simply, "and you are stupid not to have seen him before."

The profile of the mysterious doctor was in fact outlined very sharply at a table, amply served and covered with bottles and flowers, around which half a score of persons, men and women, had taken their places.

Without turning his head, Juve remarked:

"Judging by the action of the person who is at this moment lighting a cigar the supper is not far from coming to an end."

"Come, now, Juve, have you eyes in your back? How can you know what is going on at Doctor Chaleck's table, while you are looking in the opposite direction?"

Juve handed his eye-glass to the journalist.

"Ah! Now I see! A trick eye-glass, with a mirror in it — not a bad idea."

"It is quite simple," murmured Juve. "The main thing is to have thought of it. Come, let us go down."

"What? And desert the doctor?"

"An arrest should never be made in a public place when it can be avoided. Here, give me your card that I may send it up with mine."

Juve called M. Dominique, the manager, and, pointing out Chaleck to him, said:

"M. Dominique, please give our cards to that gentleman and say that we are waiting outside to speak to him."

In a few moments Chaleck came out of the saloon to the Place Pigalle.

His face was calm and his glance unmoved. Juve laid his hand upon the doctor's shoulder, and, signalling to a subordinate in uniform, cried:

"Doctor Chaleck, I arrest you in the name of the law."

Chaleck quietly flicked off his cigar ash and smiled:

"Do you know, M. Juve, I am not pleased with you. I read in the papers, during a recent holiday abroad, that you had pulled my house absolutely to pieces! That was not nice of you, when we had been on such good terms."

This speech was so startling, so unlooked for, that Juve, though not easily surprised, had nothing to answer for the moment.

Meanwhile, Chaleck tamely let himself be dragged toward the station in the Rue Rochefoucauld.

"The fine fellow," thought Juve, "must have got his whole case prepared — he will give us a run for our money; still it must — — "

The detective gave vent to a loud yell. They had just got to the point where the Rue Rochefoucauld is intersected by the Rue Notre Dame de Lorette: a cab drawn by a big horse was moving in one direction and a motor-bus coming from another. It had already cleared the Rue Pigalle, and in a second would cut across the Rue Rochefoucauld, when Chaleck, literally coming out of the Inverness coat he wore, leaped ahead of Juve, dodged under the cab horse and boarded the bus, which rapidly went on its way. All this had been accomplished in an instant.

Left dumbfounded, face to face, Juve and Fandor, together with the officer, contemplated the only token left them by Chaleck. An elegant Inverness cloak with capes, which, oddly enough, had shoulders and arms — arms of India-rubber, so well imitated that through the cloth they distinctly gave the impression of human arms.

Juve let fly a tremendous oath, then turned to Fandor and cried:

"How about Loupart?"

The two men hastily reascended the Rue Pigalle. They counted on standing sentry again before the "Crocodile." But as they reached the square Juve and Fandor were faced by fresh surprises. A powerful motor-car was slowly getting under way. In it was the American Dixon, with Josephine beside him.

Was the girl playing them false? That was the most important thing to ascertain.

The car made off at a good pace toward the Place Clichy. Half a moment later Juve was bowling after them in a taxi, calling to Fandor as he left:

"Look after the other."

Fandor understood "The other" referred to Loupart, and carefully pumped M. Dominique, but could get no further news from him, so, after waiting an hour for Juve to return, he went home to bed far from easy in his mind.

Juve followed the American through Billancourt, past Sèvres Bridge, and finally into the Bellevue District, when, opposite Brimboison Park, Dixon, with the air of a proprietor, took his motor into a fine looking estate. Then, having housed the car, the pugilist, with Loupart's mistress, went into the house, which was lit up for half an hour, after which all was plunged again into darkness.

Juve had left his taxi at the bottom of the hill, and, having cleared the low wall of the grounds, hid himself in view of the house. He waited until daybreak, but nothing occurred to trouble the peace and hush of the night. And then, unwilling to be seen in his evening clothes by chance passers-by, he regretfully returned to the Rue Bonaparte.

XXII
THE PUGILIST'S WHIM

An old servant had brought out the early coffee to the arbour in the garden. It was about eight o'clock, and in the shady retreat the freshness of springtime reigned. Soon down the gravel walk appeared the well-built figure of Dixon, dressed in white flannels. He bent under the arch of greenery that led to the arbour, and seemed vexed to find that it was empty.

Clearly the pugilist was not going to breakfast alone and, to while away the time until his companion should appear, he lighted a cigarette.

Suddenly the door of the house opened to give passage to a gracious apparition — Josephine. Wrapped in a kimona of bright silk and smiling at the fine morning, the young woman came slowly down the steps and then stopped short, blushing. Some one came to meet her — it was Dixon.

The giant, too, seemed moved. Lowering his eyes he asked:

"How are you this morning, fair lady?"

"And you, M. Dixon?"

"Mlle. Finette, the coffee is served, won't you join me?"

The two young people broke their fast in silence, exchanging only monosyllables, to ask for a napkin, a plate, the sugar. At last, overcoming his bashfulness Dixon asked in a voice full of entreaty:

"Will you always be so hard-hearted?"

Josephine, embarrassed, evaded the question, and with a show of gaiety to hide her confusion, remarked:

"This is an awfully nice place of yours."

The pugilist answered her by describing the calm and simple delights of a country life in the springtime, and, slipping his arm round her supple waist, asked her softly:

"As you consented to come this far with me, why did you repel me afterwards? Why resist me so stubbornly?"

"I was a trifle tipsy yesterday," she replied. "I don't know what I did or why I came here with you." And then, with a touch of sadness: "Naturally, finding me in such a place you took me for a — — "

"Sure enough," replied the American, "but I can see you are not like the others."

"And what attracts me to you," continued Josephine, "is that you are not a brute. Why, yesterday evening, if you had wanted, when we were alone together, eh?"

And she gave Dixon such a queer look that he asked himself whether she did not regard him as absurd for having respected her.

"I like you very much," he said, "more than any other woman. In a month from now I shall be off to America. I have already a good deal of money and I shall earn much more out there. If you will come with me, we won't part any more. Do you agree?"

Josephine was at first amused by this downright declaration, but gradually she took it more seriously. She would see the world, be elegant, rich, well dressed. She would have her future secured and no more bother with the police. But, on the other hand, it might become terribly boring after the exciting life she had led. And there was Loupart. Certainly he was often repellant to her, but he had only to come back and speak to her to be again submissive, loving and tractable. And, strange to say, there was also — just of late — at the bottom of Josephine's heart, a feeling of friendship, almost affection, for the stern and thorough-going detective, for Juve, to whom she owed her escape from a very bad fix. Fandor, too, she liked pretty well. She valued the daring journalist, quick, full of courage, and yet a good sort, free from prejudice. The more she thought about it, the more Josephine felt herself to be strikingly complex: she felt that she could not analyse her feelings, she was incomprehensible even to herself.

"Let me think it over a little longer," she asked. Dixon rose ceremoniously.

"Dear friend," he declared, "you are at home here, as long as you care to stay, and I hope you will consent to lunch with me at one o'clock. From now till then I shall leave you alone to think at your leisure."

The old servant, too, having gone off shopping, Josephine remained alone in the place, and after visiting the charming villa from top to bottom strolled delightedly amid the lovely scenery of the park. As she was about to turn into a narrow path, she uttered a loud cry. Loupart was before her. The leader of the Gang of Cyphers had his evil look and savage smile.

"How goes it?" he cried, then queried, sardonically: "Which would madame prefer, the pig-sticker or the barker?"

Josephine, in terror, stepped backwards till she rested against the trunk of a great tree.

Loupart carelessly got out his revolver and his knife: he seemed to hesitate which weapon to use.

"Loupart," stammered Josephine, in a choking voice, "don't kill me — what have I done?"

The ruffian snarled.

"Not only do you peach to M. Juve, but you let yourself be carried off by the first toff that comes along; you don't stick at making me a cuckold! That's very well!"

Josephine fell on her knees in the thick grass. Sure enough she had played Loupart false, and suddenly a wave of remorse rose in her heart. She was overcome at the thought that she could have endangered her lover even for a moment, that she could have informed the police. She was honestly maddened by the thought that Loupart had all but been arrested through her fault. Yes, he was right in reproaching her, she deserved to be punished. As for having wronged him, that was not true. She protested with all her might against his accusation of unfaithfulness.

"I was wrong in listening to the pugilist, in coming here, but in spite of appearances — Loupart, believe me, I am still worthy of you."

Loupart shrugged his shoulders.

"Well, we'll leave that for the moment. Just now you are going to obey me without a word or protest."

Josephine's heart stopped; she knew these preambles. She tried to turn the conversation.

"And how did you get here?"

"How did you get here yourself?"

"M. Dixon's motor-car."

"And who tracked you?"

"Why — no one."

"No one?" jeered the ruffian. "Then what was Juve doing in the taxi which was rolling after you?"

Josephine uttered an exclamation of surprise. Loupart went on, greatly satisfied with himself:

"And what was Loupart up to? That crafty gentleman was cosily ensconced on the springs behind the taxi in which the worthy inspector was riding."

The ruffian was teasing, and that showed he was in good humour again. Josephine put her arms round his neck and hugged him.

"It's you that I love and you alone — let's go, take me away, won't you?"

Loupart freed himself from the embrace.

"Since you are at home here — the American said as much — I must see to profiting by it. You will stay here till this evening: at five you will be at the markets, and so shall I. You won't recognise me, but I shall speak to you, and then you will tell me exactly where this pugilist locks up his swag. I want a full plan of the house, the print of the keys, all the usual truck. This evening I shall have something new for Juve and his crew, an affair in which you will serve me."

Josephine, panting, did not pay heed to this last sentence. She flushed crimson, perspiration broke out on her forehead, a great agony tightened her heart. She, so docile till then, so devoted, suddenly felt an immense scruple, an awful shame at the thought of being guilty of what her lover demanded. Against any other man, she would have obeyed, but to act in that way toward Dixon, who had treated her so considerately, she felt was beyond her powers. Here Josephine showed herself truly a woman. While determined not to be false to Loupart, she would not leave the pugilist with an evil memory of her. She hesitated to betray him and unwittingly proved the truth of the philosopher's dictum: "The most honest of women, though unwilling to give hope, is never sorry to leave behind her a regret!"

But Loupart was not going to stay discussing such subtleties with his mistress. He never gave his orders twice. To seal the reconciliation he imprinted a hasty kiss on Josephine's cheek and vanished. A sound of crackling marked his passage through the thickets. Josephine was once more alone in the great park around the villa.

Fandor and Dixon were taking tea in the drawing-room. The journalist came, he alleged, to interview Dixon about his fight with Joe Sans, the negro champion of the Soudan, which was to come off next day. After getting various details as to weight, diet and other trifles, Fandor inquired with a smile:

"But to keep in good form, Dixon, you must be as sober as a camel, as chaste as a monk, eh?"

The American smiled. Fandor had told him a few moments before that he had seen him supping at the "Crocodile" with a pretty woman.

At Juve's instigation Fandor had alleged a sporting interview, in order to get into the American's house and discover if Josephine was still there. He meant to ascertain what the relations were between the pugilist and the girl.

The allusion to that evening loosened the American's tongue. Absorbed by the pleasing impression which his pretty partner had made on him, Dixon began talking on the subject. He belonged to that class of men who, when they are in love, want the whole world to know it.

The American set the young woman on such a pedestal of innocence and purity — that Fandor wondered if the pugilist were not laughing at him. But Dixon, quite unconscious, did not conceal his intention to elope with Josephine and shortly take her to America. Suddenly he rose.

"Come," he said, "I will introduce you to her."

Fandor was about to protest, but the American was already scouring the house and searching the park, calling:

"Finette, Mlle. Finette, Josephine!"

Presently he returned, his face distorted, unnerved, dejected, and in a toneless voice he ejaculated painfully:

"The pretty little woman has made off without a word to me. I am very much grieved!"

Five minutes later, Fandor jumped into a train which took him back to Paris.

XXIII
"STATES EVIDENCE"

"Juve, I've been fooled." The journalist was resting on the great couch in his friend's study, Rue Bonaparte, and wound up with this assertion the long account of the fruitless inquiry he had made at Dixon's.

"I'm played out! For two days I haven't stopped a minute. After the night at the "Crocodile," which I spent for the most part, as I told you, in search of Loupart, yesterday my day went in fruitless trips; my mind is made up; to-night I shall do no more!"

"A cigarette, Fandor?"

"Thanks."

From the crystal vase where Juve, an inveterate smoker, always kept an ample stock of tobacco, he chose an Egyptian cigarette.

"My dear Juve, it is absolutely necessary to go again to Sèvres and draw a close net round Dixon. He needs watching. Isn't that your opinion?"

"I'm not sure."

Juve thought for a few moments, then:

"After all, what grounds have you for thinking that Dixon should be watched?"

"Why, any number of reasons."

"What are they?"

It was Fandor's turn to be surprised. He had given Juve the account of his visit, supposing that would bring him to his way of thinking, and now Juve doubted Dixon being a suspect.

"You ask me for particulars. I am going to reply with generalisations. Taking it all in all, what do we know of Dixon? That he was in a certain place and carried off Josephine under our very eyes. Hence he is a friend of Josephine's, which in itself looks compromising."

"Oh!" protested Juve. "You arrive at your conclusions very quickly, Fandor. Josephine is not an honest woman. She may know the type of people that haunt the night resorts, yet who, for all that, need not be murderers."

"Then, Juve, how do you account for it that during my visit Dixon tricked me and kept me from meeting Josephine while making believe to look for her? Is not that again a sign of complicity? Does not that show clearly that Josephine, realising that she is suspected in our eyes, has decided to evade us?"

Juve smiled.

"Fandor, my lad, you are endowed with a prodigious imagination. You impute to Dixon the worst intentions without any proof. He got Josephine away, you say? What makes you think so? If you did not see her it was due to collusion between them both. Why? As far as I can see, Josephine simply picked up an old lover of hers at the 'Crocodile' and went off with him as naturally as possible, preferring not to see the arrest of Loupart or of Chaleck. I admit that next day she simply took French leave of the worthy American, and you may be sure he knew nothing about her going."

Fandor was silent and Juve resumed:

"That being so, what can we bring against Dixon? Merely that he knows Josephine."

"You are right, Juve; perhaps I went too far with my deductions, but to speak frankly, I don't see clearly what we are to do now. All our trails are crossed. Loupart is in flight, Chaleck vanished, and as for Josephine, I doubt our finding her again for ever so long."

All the while the journalist was speaking, Juve had remained leaning against the window, watching the passers-by.

"Fandor, come and see! By the omnibus, there. The person who is going to cross."

The journalist burst out:

"Well, I'm damned!"

"You see, Fandor, you must never swear to anything."

"Well, ain't we going to catch and arrest her?"

"Why? Do you think her being in this street is due to chance? Look, she is crossing; she is coming straight here. She is entering the house. I tell you in a few moments Josephine will have climbed my stairs and will be seated cosily in this armchair, which I get ready and set full in the light."

Fandor could not get over his astonishment.

"Did you make an appointment with her?"

"Not at all."

Jean, the detective's servant, came into the room and announced:

"There is a lady waiting in the sitting-room. She would not give her name."

"Show her in, Jean."

A few moments later Josephine entered.

"Good day, Mademoiselle," cried Juve in a cordial tone. "What fresh news have you to tell us?"

Loupart's mistress stood in the middle of the room, somewhat taken aback. But Juve set her at ease.

"Sit down, Josephine. You mustn't mind my friend Fandor. He has just been telling me about your friend Dixon."

"You know him, sir?"

"A little," said Fandor. "And you, Mademoiselle, have been seeing something of him lately?"

"I happened to meet him at the 'Crocodile.'"

"And took a liking to him?"

"We took a liking to each other." She turned to Juve. "I suppose you distrust me for giving you the slip with another man?"

Juve smiled. "You found a good companion and forgot us. There is really nothing to be angry about. Now, won't you tell us what brings you here?"

"Yes, but M. Juve, you must swear to me that you will never repeat what I am going to tell you."

"It is very serious then?"

"M. Juve, I am going to put you in the way of arresting Loupart."

"You are very kind, my dear Josephine, but if the attempt is to succeed no better than that we made at the 'Crocodile' — — "

"No, no, this time you'll be sure to nab him. Day after to-morrow at 2 o'clock, Loupart is going with some of his gang to Nogent, 7 Rue des Charmilles. He has a job there under way."

Juve laughed. "They've been fooling you, Josephine. Isn't that your view, Fandor? Do you think that Loupart would try a stroke in broad daylight?"

Josephine gave more details, eager to persuade him.

"There will be fifteen of them outside a little house whose tenants are away. Some of them will make a crowd to help their mates in case of danger. The Beard is to be in it, too."

"And Loupart?"

"Yes, Loupart, I tell you. He will wear a black mask by which you can identify him."

"Very well, if we have nothing better to do we will take a trip to Nogent day after to-morrow; eh, Fandor?"

"As you like, Juve."

"Only, remember this, my dear Josephine, if you are putting up a game on us you'll be sorry for it. There is a way, to be sure, in which you can prove your good faith. Be at Nogent Station at half-past one. If we find Loupart where you say he will be, we shall arrest him; if we don't find him — — "

The detective paused, significantly.

"You will nab him. Only we mustn't look as if we met by appointment. No one must suspect that I gave you the tip."

Hereupon, Josephine started to go. Her manoeuvre had succeeded, and Loupart's business would go ahead safely. She turned at the door and nodded, looking at Fandor.

"Another thing; Loupart doesn't love you; you had better be on your guard."

Juve turned thoughtfully to Fandor:

"Strange! Is this woman playing with us, or is she in earnest, and how she looked at you when telling us to be on our guard!"

XXIV
A MYSTERIOUS CLASP

"Hullo! Hullo!"

Waking with a start, Juve rushed to the telephone. It was already broad daylight, but the detective had gone to bed very late and had been sleeping profoundly.

"Yes, it's I, Juve. The Sûreté? It's you, M. Havard? Yes, I am free. Oh! That's strange. No signs? I understand. Count on me. I'll go there and keep you informed."

Juve dressed in haste, went down to the street and hailed a taxi.

"To Sèvres, the foot of the hill at Bellevue, and look sharp about it!"

Juve left his taxi-cab, and mounted the slope on foot to the elegant villa inhabited by Dixon. All was quiet, and if he had not had word, the detective would have doubted that he was close to the scene of a crime, or at least of an attempted one.

Scarcely had he entered the grounds when a sergeant came toward him and saluted. Juve inquired:

"What has happened?"

"M. Dixon is resting just now, and the doctor has forbidden the least noise."

"Is his condition serious?"

"I think not from what Doctor Plassin says."

"Now, Sergeant, tell me everything from the beginning."

The sergeant drew Juve to the arbour, where a policeman was seated making out a report. Juve took the paper and read:

"We, the undersigned, Dubois, Sergeant in the second squad of foot-police, quartered at Sèvres, together with Constable Verdier, received this morning, June 28th, at 6.35 from M. Olivetti, a business man, living in Bellevue, the following declaration:

"Having left my home at 6.15 and being on the way to the State Railway to take the 6.42 train, by which I go every day to my work, I was passing the slopes of Bellevue, when, being level with Brimborion Park, a little short of the villa number 16, which I hear belongs to M. Dixon, an American pugilist, I heard a revolver shot followed by the noise of breaking glass, the pieces falling on to a hard ground, most likely stone.

"Having halted for a moment through caution, I looked to see if anyone was hiding near by. I saw nothing but heard three more revolver shots in quick succession, seeming to come from Dixon's house. After some minutes I went near the house and ascertained that the panes of the window on the right side of the front were broken, and the pieces strewed the asphalt terrace in front of the house.

" 'I made up my mind to ring, but no one opened the door. I then thought that some prowlers had amused themselves by making a shindy, and I was about to continue to the train when I thought I heard faint cries coming from the inside of the house. Then, fearing there was a mishap or a crime, I ran to the police station and made the above statement in presence of the sergeant.' "

Juve turned to the sergeant, who gave further details.

"Constable Verdier and I immediately hastened here. We reached the terrace of the house, but there we came to a closed door we could not break in. Having shouted loudly we were answered by groans and cries for help which came from the room on the first floor of which the windows were broken. We then got a ladder and climbed up. I passed my hand inside and worked the hasp of the window. We went in and found ourselves in a bedroom in apple-pie order and in which nothing appeared to have been disarranged."

"And on a second inspection?" queried Juve.

"I went to the far end of the room and found stretched on the bed a man in undress, who seemed a prey to violent pains. I learned afterwards that this was M. Dixon, the tenant of the house. He could scarcely utter a word or move. His shoulders and arms were out of the clothes, and I could discern that the skin of his chest and shoulders bore traces of blood effusion. On a bracket to the right of the bed lay a revolver, the six cartridges of which had been recently fired."

"Ah!" cried Juve. "And then?"

"I thought the first thing to do was to call in a doctor. M. Olivetti consented to go and call Doctor Plassin, who lives near by. Five minutes later the doctor came, and I took advantage of his presence to send my man to the Station."

"Have you been over the house?"

"Not yet, Inspector, but nothing will be easier, for in turning out the pockets of the victim's clothes we found his bunch of keys."

"To bring the doctor into the house, you must have opened the door to him, and therefore had a glimpse of the other rooms in the house, the lobby, the staircase?"

The sergeant shook his head.

"No, Inspector. We went up the ladder. I tried to get out of the door of M. Dixon's room, but found it was locked. This seemed strange, for the assailant presumably entered by the door."

"By the by, Sergeant, are there no servants here? The place seems deserted."

Constable Verdier put in his word:

"The American lives here alone except for an old charwoman who comes in before nine. She will probably be here in half an hour, for she can have no idea of what has happened."

"Good," said Juve. "You will let me know as soon as she comes; wait for her in the garden. As for us," and he turned to the sergeant, "let us make our way inside."

The two, armed with Dixon's keys, opened without difficulty the main entrance door to the ground floor. There they found nothing out of the way, but on reaching the first floor, the marks of some one's passage was clearly visible.

The door of a lumber room stood wide open, and on its floor sheets of paper, letters and documents lay scattered about. Juve took a candle and, after a brief investigation, exclaimed:

"They were after the strong box."

A large steel safe, built into the wall, had been burst open, and the workman-like manner in which it had been done showed clearly the hand of an expert. Juve carefully examined the floor, picked up two or three papers that had evidently been trodden on, took some measurements which he jotted down in his note-book, and, without telling the sergeant his conclusions, went downstairs again, paying no heed to the next room in which Dixon lay, watched over by Doctor Plassin.

Verdier, who was mounting guard before the house, came forward and said:

"Mr. Inspector, the doctor says M. Dixon is awake. Do you care to see him?"

Juve at once had the ladder put to the first story window and made his way into the pugilist's room. The men's description was correct. No disorder reigned in the chamber, at the far end of which, on a great brass bed, a sturdy individual, his face worn with suffering, lay stretched.

In two words Juve introduced himself to the doctor; then expressed his sorrow for Dixon's plight.

"These are only contusions, M. Juve. Serious enough, but nothing more. By the by, M. Dixon may congratulate himself upon owning muscles of exceptional vigour. Otherwise, from the grip he must have undergone, his body would be no more than a shapeless pulp."

Juve pricked up his ears. He had heard before of bones snapped and broken under a strain that neither flesh nor muscle could resist. The mysterious death of Lady Beltham at once occurred to his memory.

"Mr. Dixon, you will tell me all the details of the tragic night you have passed through. You probably dined in Paris last evening?"

The sick man replied in a fairly firm voice:

"No, sir, I dined at home alone."

"Is that your usual habit?"

"No, sir, but between five and seven I had been training hard for my match which was to have come off to-morrow with Joe Sans."

"Do you think your opponent would have been capable of trying to injure you to keep you out of the ring?"

"No, Joe Sans is a good sportsman; besides, he lives at Brussels, and isn't due in Paris till to-morrow."

"And after dinner, what did you do?"

"I fastened the shutters and doors, came up here and undressed."

"Are you in the habit of bolting yourself into your room?"

"Yes, I lock my door every evening."

"What time was it when you went to bed?"

"Ten at latest."

"And then?"

"Then I went fast asleep, but in the middle of the night I was waked by a strange noise. It sounded like a scratching at my door. I gave a shout and banged my fist on the partition."

"Why?" asked Juve, surprised.

The American explained:

"I thought the scratching came from rats, and I simply made a noise to frighten them away. Then, the sound having ceased, I fell asleep again."

"And afterwards?"

"I was waked again by the sound of stealthy footsteps on the landing of the first floor."

"This time you went to see?"

"I meant to do so, I was about to get up. I had put out my arm to get my matches and revolver, when suddenly I felt a weight on my bed and then I was corded, bound like a sausage, my arms tight to my body! For ten minutes I struggled with all the power of my muscles against a frightful and mysterious grip which continually grew tighter."

"A lasso!" suggested Doctor Plassin in a low voice.

"Were you able to determine the nature of the thing that was gripping you?" asked Juve.

"I don't know. I remember feeling at the touch of the thing a marked sensation of dampness and cold."

"A wetted lasso, exactly. A rope dipped in water tautens of itself," remarked the doctor.

"You had to make a great effort to prevent being crushed or broken?"

"A more than human effort, Mr. Inspector, as the doctor has witnessed; if I had not muscles of steel and exceptional strength I should have been flattened."

"Good — good," applauded Juve. "That's exactly it!"

"Really! You think so?" queried the American with a touch of sarcasm.

Juve smilingly apologised. His approval meant no more than that the statements of the victim coincided with the theories he had formed. And indeed he saw clearly in the unsuccessful attempt on the American and the achieved killing of Lady Beltham a common way of going to work, the same process. Undoubtedly the American owed it to his robust physique that he got off but slightly scathed, whereas the hapless woman had been totally crushed.

The similarity of the two crimes allowed Juve to make further inductions. He reckoned that it was not by chance that Dixon had met Josephine at the "Crocodile" two nights before, while the presence of both Chaleck and Loupart in that establishment was still less accidental. And already he felt pleased at the thought that he knew almost to a certainty the villains to whom this fresh crime must be ascribed. They had wanted to get rid of Dixon, that was sure, and by a process still unknown to Juve, but which he would soon discover. They had rendered the pugilist helpless while they were robbing him.

"Had you a large sum of money in your safe?" he asked.

The American gave a violent start.

"They've burgled me! Tell me, sir, tell me quickly!"

Juve nodded in the affirmative. Dixon stammered feebly:

"Four thousand pounds! They've taken four thousand pounds from me! I received the sum a few days ago!"

"Gently, gently!" observed the doctor. "You will make yourself feverish and I shall have to stop the interview."

Juve put in:

"I only want a few moments more, doctor. It is important." Then, turning to Dixon, he resumed: "How did your struggle with the mysterious pressure end?"

"After about ten minutes I felt my bands relaxing. In a short while I was free; I heard no more, but suffered such great pain that I fell back in bed and either slept or fainted."

"Then you did not get up at all?"

"No."

"And the door of your room to the landing remained locked all night?"

"Yes, all night."

"How about this broken glass in your window? Those revolver shots at six in the morning?"

"It was I, firing from my bed to make a noise and bring some one here."

"I thought as much," said Juve, as he went down on all fours and proceeded to examine the carpeting of the room between the bed and the door, a distance of some seven feet. The carpet, of very close fabric, afforded no trace, but on a white bearskin rug the detective noted in places tufts of hair glued together as if something moist and sticky had passed over it. He cut off one of these tufts and shut it carefully in his pocketbook. He then went to the door which was hidden by a velvet curtain. He could not suppress a cry of amazement. In the lower panel of the door a round hole had been made about six or eight inches in diameter. It was four inches above the floor, and might have been made for a cat.

"Did you have that hole made in the door?" asked Juve.

"No. I don't know what it is," replied the American.

"Neither do I," rejoined Juve, "but I have an idea." Doctor Plassin was jubilant.

"There you are!" he cried. "A lasso! And it was thrust in by that hole."

Through the window, Verdier called:

"M. Inspector, the charwoman is coming."

Juve looked at his watch.

"Half-past nine. I will see her in a minute."

XXV
THE TRAP

"Twelve o'clock! Hang it! I've just time to get there to keep my engagement with Josephine."

Juve was going down Belleville hill as fast as his legs could take him by a short cut past the Sèvres school. He cast a mocking glance toward the little police station which stands smart and trim at one side of the high road.

"Pity," he murmured, "that I can't escort my friends to that delightful country house."

Then he hastened his pace still more. He was growing angry.

"I told Fandor to be at Nogent Station exactly at 1.30. It is now five past twelve and I am still at Sèvres. Matters are getting complicated. Oh, I'll take the tramway to Versailles' gate. From there I'll drive to Nogent Station in a taxi."

He put this plan into execution, and was lucky enough to find a place in the Louvre-Versailles' tram.

"All things considered, I have not wasted my morning. Poor Dixon! He was lucky to get off so cheaply. It would seem now that Josephine told the truth in saying he is not an accomplice of the Gang."

Juve reflected a while, then added:

"Only it looks as if that accursed Josephine had put her friends up to the job."

At the St. Cloud gate the tram came to a stop and Juve got down, hailed a taxi, and told the driver:

"To Nogent Station and look sharp. I'm in a terrible hurry."

The driver nodded assent, Juve got in, and the vehicle started. The taxi had hardly been going five minutes when Juve became impatient.

"Go quicker, my man! Don't you know how to drive?"

The man replied, nettled:

"I don't want to get run in for breaking the regulations."

Juve laughed.

"Never mind the regulations, I'm from Police Headquarters."

The magical word took effect. From that moment, heedless of the frantic signals of policemen, the driver tore along at full speed and reached the square in front of Nogent Station.

"It is only 1.45 — Fandor should just have got here."

Juve, indeed, had only just settled with his driver when Fandor popped up from the waiting-room.

"Well, Juve! Anything fresh this morning?"

The detective smiled.

"Any number of things. But I'll tell you later. Where is Josephine?"

"Not here yet."

"The deuce!"

"That confirms my suspicions; eh, Juve?"

"Somewhat. I should be astonished if we did see her."

The detective led the journalist away, and the two went for a turn beside the railway-line on the deserted boulevard.

"Fandor, this is the time to draw up a plan of action. Do you remember the directions Josephine gave us?"

"Vaguely."

"Well, we are now going to the neighbourhood of the Rue des Charmilles. It is number 7 that Loupart and his gang are to loot, according to Josephine. Yesterday afternoon I sent my men to look at the street; this is how they described it to me. It is a sort of lane with no issue; the house which we are concerned with is the last, standing on the right. It is a lodge of humble aspect, the tenants of which are really away. There are not many people living in this Charmilles Lane, and the place is well chosen for such a job, at least that is Michel's opinion.

"Oh, I forgot one thing, round the house is a fairly large garden of which the walls are luckily high. So it is likely that even if the burglars should discover our presence they could not get off the back way."

"And what is your plan of action, Juve?"

"A very simple one. We are going to the entry of the Rue Charmilles and wait there. When our men come up with us I shall try to pick out Loupart and fly at his throat. There will be a struggle, no doubt, but in the meantime you must bellow with all your might: 'Murder' and 'Help.' I trust that succour will reach us."

"Then you haven't any plain-clothes men here?"

"No. I don't want to let my superiors know about this expedition."

The two men went forward some paces in silence along an empty side street, till Juve halted in a shady corner and drew out his Browning, carefully seeing to the magazine.

"Do as I do, Fandor"; he prepared for a tussle. "I smell powder in the air."

Juve was about to start forward again when suddenly a tremendous uproar broke out: "Help! Help!"

Juve seized Fandor by the arm.

"Take the left-hand pavement!"

The two had just reached the corner of the street where the house spoken of by Josephine should stand, when a jostling crowd of people came in sight, rushing toward them, uttering shouts and yells. Juve and Fandor recognised a man fleeing at full speed in front of them, whose face was hidden by a black mask! Behind him two other men were running, also masked, but with grey velvet. In the crowd following were grocers' assistants, workmen of all kinds, even a Nogent policeman.

"Help! Murder! Arrest him!"

The fleeing man was threatening his pursuers with an enormous revolver.

"Look out!" shouted Juve. "Loupart is mine! You tackle the others!"

But suddenly catching sight of the detective Loupart slackened his pace.

"Get out of the way!" he cried, flourishing his revolver.

"Stop, or I fire!" returned Juve.

"Fire then! I, too, shall fire!" And, leaping toward the detective, the outlaw pointed his revolver at him and fired twice.

With a quick movement Juve leaped aside. The bullets must have brushed him, but luckily he was not touched. The plucky detective again flung himself on Loupart, seized him by the collar and tried to throw him down.

"Let me go! I'll do for you —— "

For a moment Juve felt the cold muzzle of the weapon on his neck. Then, with a supreme effort, he forced the outlaw's hands down and, aiming his revolver, fired.

"Help! I —I —— "

A gush of blood welled up from the ruffian's collar. He turned twice, and then fell heavily on the ground.

In the meantime Fandor was struggling with the two men in the grey masks. Juve was about to go to his assistance, when the crowd now made a rush and the detective became the central point of a furious encounter: blows and kicks rained on him. He succumbed to numbers.

It was now Fandor's turn to help his friend, and he was about to join the fight when he stood rooted to the spot in utter amazement. A little beyond the groups of struggling men he caught sight of an individual standing beside a tripod on which was placed a contrivance he did not at once identify. The man seemed greatly amused, and was watching the scene laughing and showing no desire to intervene.

"Very good! Very good! That will make a splendid film!"

Fandor understood ——

His head bandaged and his arm in a sling, Juve was replying in a shaky voice to the Super-intendent of Police of Nogent.

"No, Superintendent, I realised nothing. It is monstrous! I asked in the most perfect good faith. I did not fire till I had been fired at three times."

"You didn't notice the strange get-up of the burglars? And of the policemen? Of that poor actor, Bonardin, you half killed?"

Juve shook his head.

"I hadn't time to notice details. I want you to understand, Superintendent, how things came about, to realise how the trap was laid for me....I came to Nogent, assured that I was about to face dangerous ruffians. I was to encounter them at such an hour, in such a street. I was given their description: they would have their faces masked and come out of a certain house. And it all happened as described. I hadn't gone ten paces in the said street when sure enough I saw people rushing toward me bawling 'Help.' I recognised men in masks: had I time to look at the details of their costumes? Certainly not! I spring at the throat of the fugitive. He has a revolver and fires. How could I know the weapon was only loaded blank? He, an actor in a cinematograph scene, takes me for another, acting the part of a policeman. He fires at me and I retaliate."

"And you half kill him."

"For which I am exceedingly sorry. But nothing could lead me to suspect a trap."

"It's lucky you didn't wound anyone else. How did matters end?"

"The actors, naturally enough, were furious with me, and I was being roughly handled when the real policemen arrived and rescued me. All was explained when I brought out my card of identity. While they were taking me to the station, the actor Bonardin was being carried to the nearest house, a convent, I believe."

"Yes, the Convent of the Ladies of St. Clotilde."

The trap had been well devised, and Juve was not wrong in saying that anyone in his place would have been taken in by it. And so while the detective was detained at the station, Fandor, after a long and minute interrogation, returned to Paris in a state of deep dejection.

XXVI
AT THE HOUSE OF BONARDIN, THE ACTOR

In the Place d'Anvers, Fandor was passing Rokin College. He heard some one calling him. "Monsieur Fandor! Monsieur Fandor!"

It was Josephine, breathless and panting, her bright eyes glowing with joy.

Fandor turned, astonished.

"What is up?"

Josephine paused a second, then taking Fandor's hand familiarly drew him into the square, which at this time of day was almost deserted.

"Oh, it's something out of the common, I can assure you. I am going to astonish you!"

"You've done that already. The mere sight of you —— "

"You thought I was arrested, didn't you?"

Fandor nodded.

"Well, it's your Juve who is jugged!"

Contrary to Josephine's expectation, Fandor did not appear very astonished.

"Come now, Miss Josephine, that's a likely tale! Juve arrested? On what grounds?"

Josephine began an incoherent story.

"I tell you they squabbled like rag-pickers! 'You make justice ridiculous,' shouted Fuselier. 'No one has the right to commit such blunders!' Well, they kept going on like that for a quarter of an hour. And then Fuselier rang and two Municipal guards came and he said: 'Arrest that man there!' pointing to Juve. And your friend the detective was obliged to let them do it. Only as he left the room he gave Fuselier such a look! Believe me, between those two it is war to the death from now."

When she had ended Fandor asked in a calm voice:

"And how did you get away, Josephine?"

"Oh, M. Fuselier was very nice. 'It's you again?' said he when he saw me. 'To be sure it is,' answered I, 'and I'm glad to meet you again, M. Magistrate.' Then he began to hold forth about the cinema business. I told him what I knew about it, what I told you. Loupart stuffed me up with his tale of a trap. As sure as my name's Josephine I believed what my lover told me."

Fandor gave her a penetrating glance.

"And how about the Dixon business?"

Josephine coloured, and said in a low tone:

"Oh, the Dixon business, as to that — we are very good pals, Dixon and I. Just fancy, I went to see him yesterday afternoon. He has taken a fancy to me. He promised to keep me in luxury. Ah, if I dared," sighed the girl.

"You would do well to leave Loupart."

"Leave Loupart? Especially now that Juve is in quod, Loupart will be the King of Paris!"

"Do you think your lover will attach much weight to the arrest of Juve? Won't he fancy it's a put-up job?"

"A put-up job! How could it be? Why, I saw with my two eyes Juve led away with the bracelets on his wrists."

The growing hubbub of the newsboys crying the evening papers drew near the Place d'Anvers. Instinctively Fandor, followed by Josephine, went toward them. On the boulevard he bought a paper.

"There you see!" cried Josephine triumphantly. "Here it is in print, so it is true!"

In scare headlines appeared this notice — "Amazing development in the affair of the Outlaws of La Chapelle. Detective Juve under lock and key."

Fandor, when he met Josephine in the Place d'Anvers, was on his way to the Rue des Abesses where Bonardin occupied a nice little suite of three rooms, tastefully decorated and comfortably furnished.

The actor had his shoulder in plaster — Juve's bullet had broken his clavicle, but the doctor declared that with a few days' rest he would be quite well again.

"M. Fandor, I am very sorry for what is happening to M. Juve. Do you think if I were to declare my intention not to proceed against him —— "

Fandor cut his companion short.

"Let justice take its course, M. Bonardin. There will always be time later on."

Although M. Bonardin was only twenty-five, he was beginning to have some reputation. By hard work he had come rapidly to the front, and was fast gaining a position among the best interpreters of modern comedy.

"My dream," he exclaimed to Fandor, "is one day to attain to the fame of my masters, of such men as Tazzide, Gémier, Valgrand and Du600ény."

"You knew Valgrand?" asked Fandor.

Bonardin smiled.

"Why, we were great friends. When I first made my appearance at the theatre, after the Conservatoire, Valgrand was my model, my master. You certainly don't recollect it, M. Fandor, but I played the lover in the famous play 'La Toche Sanglante,' for which Valgrand had made himself up exactly like Gurn, the murderer of Lord Beltham. You must have heard of the case?"

Fandor pretended to tax his memory.

"Why, to be sure I do recall certain incidents, but won't you refresh my memory?"

Bonardin asked no better than to chatter.

"Valgrand, on the first night of his presentation of Gurn, was quite worn out and left the theatre very late. He did not come again! For the second performance, his understudy took his part. The following day they sent to Valgrand's rooms; he had not been there for two days. The third day from the 'first night' Valgrand came among us again."

"Pray go on, you interest me immensely!"

"Valgrand came back, but he had gone mad. He managed to get to his dressing-room after taking the wrong door. 'I don't know a single word of my part,' he confessed to me. I comforted him as best I could, but he flung himself down on his couch and shook his head helplessly at me. 'I have been very ill, Bonardin,' then suddenly he demanded: 'Where is Charlot?'

"Charlot was his dresser. I remembered now that Charlot had not returned to the theatre since his master's disappearance. His body was found later in the Rue Messier. He had been murdered. I did not want to mention this to him for fear it might upset him still more, so I advised my old friend to wait for me till the end of the play and let me keep him company. I intended to take him home and fetch a doctor. Valgrand assented readily. I was then obliged to leave him hurriedly: they were calling me — it was my cue. When I returned Valgrand had vanished: he had left the theatre. We were not to see him again!"

"A sad affair," commented Fandor.

Bonardin continued his narrative:

"Shortly afterwards in a deserted house in the Rue Messier, near Boulevard Arago, the police found the body of a murdered man. The corpse was easily identified; it was that of Charlot, Valgrand's dresser."

"How did he come there? The house had no porter: the owner, an old peasant, knew nothing."

"Well, what do you conclude from this?" asked Fandor.

"My theory is that Valgrand murdered his dresser, for some reason unknown to us. Then, overcome by his crime, he went mad and committed suicide. Of that there is no doubt."

"Oh!" muttered Fandor, a little taken aback by this unexpected assertion.

The journalist, though he had closely followed the actor's account, was far from drawing the same conclusions. For in fact, Gurn, Lord Beltham's murderer, whom Fandor believed to be Fantômas, had certainly got Valgrand executed in his stead. The Valgrand who came back to the theatre, three days after the execution, was not the real one, but the man who had taken his place — Gurn, the criminal, Gurn — Fantômas. Ah! that was a stroke of the true Fantômas sort! It was certain that if Valgrand's disappearance had been simultaneous with Gurn's execution, there might have been suspicions. Gurn — Fantômas then found it necessary to show Valgrand living to witnesses, so that these could swear that the real Valgrand had not died instead of Gurn.

But Valgrand was an actor, Gurn — Fantômas was not! Not enough of one at least to venture to take the place on the boards of such a consummate player, such a famous tragedian.

"And that was the end?" asked Fandor.

"The end, no!" declared the actor. "Valgrand was married and had a son. As is often the case with artists, the Valgrand marriage was not a success, and madame, a singer of talent, was separated from her husband, and travelled much abroad.

"About a year after these sad occurrences I had a visit from her. On her way through Paris, she had come to draw the allowance made her by her husband, to supply not only her own wants, but also those of her son, of whom she had the custody. Mme. Valgrand chatted with me for hours together. I recounted to her at length what I have had the honour of telling you, and it seemed to me that she gave no great credence to my words.

"Not that she threw doubts on my statements, but she kept reiterating, 'That is not like him; I know Valgrand would never have behaved in such a way!'

"But I never could get her to say exactly what she thought. Some weeks after this first visit I saw her again. Matters were getting complicated. There was no certificate of her husband's death. Her men of business made his 'absence' a pretext: she no longer drew a cent of her allowance, and yet people knew that Valgrand had left a pretty large amount, and it was in the bank or with a lawyer, I forget which. You are aware, M. Fandor, that when the settling of accounts, or questions of inheritance or wills, come to the fore there is no end to them."

"That's a fact," replied Fandor.

"We must believe," went on Bonardin, "that the matter was important in Mme. Valgrand's eyes, for she refused fine offers from abroad, and planted herself in Paris, living on her savings. The good woman evidently had a double object, to recover the inheritance for her son, little René, and also to get at the truth touching her husband's fate.

"She evidently cherished the hope that her husband was not guilty of the dresser's murder, that perhaps he was not even dead, that he would get over his madness if ever they managed to find him. In short, M. Fandor, some six or seven months ago, when I had quite ceased to think of these events, I found myself face to face with Mme. Valgrand on the Boulevard. I had some difficulty in recognising her, for my friend's widow was no longer dressed like the Parisian smart woman. Her hair was plastered down and drawn tightly back, her garments were plain and humble, her dress almost neglected. No doubt the poor woman had experienced cruel disappointments.

"Good day, Mme. Valgrand,' I cried, moving toward her with outstretched hands. She stopped me with a gesture.

"'Hush,' she breathed, 'there is no Mme. Valgrand now. I am a companion.' And the unhappy woman explained that to earn her living she had to accept an inferior position as reader and housekeeper to a rich lady."

"And to whom did Mme. Valgrand go as companion?"

"To an Englishwoman, I believe, but the name escapes me."

"Mme. Valgrand wished, you say, that her identity should remain unknown? Do you know what name she took?"

"Yes — Mme. Raymond."

Some moments later Fandor left the actor and was hastening down the Rue Lepic as fast as his legs would take him.

XXVII
THE MOTHER SUPERIOR

"The Mother Superior, if you please?"

The door shut automatically upon Fandor. He was in the little inner court of the small convent, face to face with a Sister, who gazed in alarm at the unexpected guest. The journalist persisted:

"Can I see the Mother Superior?"

"Well, sir, yes — no, I think not."

The worthy nun evidently did not know what to say. Finally making up her mind she pointed to a passage, and, drawing aside to let the journalist pass, said:

"Be good enough to go in there and wait a few moments."

Fandor was ushered into a large, plain and austere room — doubtless the parlour of the community. At the windows hung long, white curtains, while before the half-dozen armchairs lay tiny rugs of matting; the floor, very waxed, was slippery to the tread. The journalist regarded curiously the walls upon which were hung here and there religious figures or chromos of an edifying kind. Above the chimney hung a great crucifix of ebony. But for the noise from without, the passing of the trains and motors, and were it not also for the fine savour of cooking and roast onions, one might have thought oneself a hundred leagues from the world in the peaceful calm of this little convent.

Fandor, on leaving Bonardin, had decided to fulfill without delay a pious mission given him by Juve's victim.

Taken in at the time of his accident by the Sisters of the Rue Charmille, Bonardin had received from them the first aid his condition required, and as he had left them without a word of thanks, he had begged Fandor to return and hand them on his behalf a fifty-franc bill for their poor.

After some minutes the door opened and a nun appeared. She greeted Fandor with a slight movement of the head; while the journalist bowed deferentially before her.

"Have I the honour of speaking to the Mother Superior?"

"Our Mother sends her excuses," murmured the nun, "for not being able to receive you at this moment. However, I can take her place, sir. I am in charge of the finances of the house."

"I bring you news, Sister."

The nun clasped her hands.

"Good news, I hope! How is the poor young man doing?"

"As well as can be expected; the ball was extracted without trouble by the doctors."

"I shall thank St. Comus, the patron saint of surgeons. And his assailant? Surely he will be well punished?"

Fandor smiled.

"His assailant was the victim of a terrible misconception. He is a most upright man."

"Then I will pray to St. Yves, the patron saint of advocates, to get him out of his difficulty."

"Well," cried Fandor, "since you have so many saints at command, Sister, you would do well to point out to me one who might favour the efforts of the police in their struggle with the ruffians."

The nun was a woman of sense who understood a joke. She rejoined: "You might try St. George, sir, the patron saint of warriors." Then becoming serious again, the Sister made an end of the interview. "Our Mother Superior will be much touched, sir, when I report the kind step you have taken in coming here to us."

"Allow me, Sister," broke in Fandor, "my mission is not over yet."

Here the journalist discreetly proffered the note.

"This is from M. Bonardin, for your poor."

The nun was profuse in her thanks, and looking at Fandor with a touch of malice:

"You may perhaps smile, sir, if I say I shall thank St. Martin, the patron saint of the charitable. In any case I shall do it with my whole heart."

The soft sound of a bell came from the distance; the Sister instinctively turned her head and looked through the windows at the inner cloister of the convent.

"The bell calls you, no doubt, Sister?" he inquired.

"It is, indeed, the hour of Vespers."

Fandor, followed by the Sister, left the parlour and reached the outer gate. Already the porter was about to open it for him when he pulled up short. Moving at a measured pace, one behind the other, the ladies of the community crossed the courtyard, going toward the chapel at the far end of the garden.

"Sister," Fandor inquired anxiously, "who is that nun who walks at the head?"

"That is our holy Mother Superior."

Fandor was lucky enough to find a taxi as he left the little convent, into which he jumped: he was immersed in such deep reflections that when the taxi stopped he was quite surprised to find himself in Rue Bonaparte, when he had meant to go up to Bonardin's and expected to reach Montmarte.

"Where did I tell you to go?" he asked the driver.

The man looked at his fare in amazement:

"To the address you gave me, I suppose."

Fandor did not reply, but paid his fare.

"Heaven inspires me," he thought. "To be sure I wanted to see Bonardin to tell him I had done his commission, but it was to prove I should have gone after what I found out at the convent."

The journalist remained motionless on the pavement without seeming to feel the jostling of the passers-by. He stood there with his eyes fixed on the ground, his mind lost in a dream. He had unconsciously gone back several years, to his mysterious childhood, stormy and restless. He went over again in thought, this last affair, which had once more brought him so intimately into Juve's life: the abominable crime in the Cité Frochot, in which Chaleck and Loupart were involved, and behind them Fantômas — the crime of which the victim — as Juve had clearly established — was no other than Lady — —

He quickly entered the house and rushed up the stairs, but halted on the landing.

"What have I come here for? If I am to believe the papers, Juve is under lock and key: It must be instinct that guides me. I feel that I am going to see Juve: besides, I must."

He did not ring, for he enjoyed the unique favour of a key which allowed him to enter Juve's place at will. He entered and went straight to the study: it was empty. He then cried out:

"Juve! Many things have happened since I had the pleasure of seeing you! Be good enough to let me into your office. I have two words to say to you."

But Fandor's words fell dead in the silence of the apartment. After this summons he made his way into the office, and ensconced himself in an armchair: clearly Fandor was assured his friend had heard him. And he was not wrong! Two seconds later, lifting a curtain that hid a secret entrance to the study, Juve appeared.

"You speak as if you knew I was here!"

The two men looked at each other and burst into shouts of laughter.

"So you understood it was all a put-up affair intended to make our opponents believe that for a time I was powerless to hurt them. What do you think of my notion?"

"First rate," replied Fandor. "The more so that the fair Josephine 'saw with her own eyes' some of the force taking you off to prison."

"Everybody believe it, don't they?"

"Everybody."

"Look here. You spoke just now as though you knew I was here?"

Fandor smiled.

"The odour of hot smoke is easily distinguished from the dankness of cold tobacco."

Juve approved.

"Well done, Fandor. Here, for your pains, roll a cigarette and let's talk. Have you anything fresh?"

"Yes — and a lot, too!"

Fandor related the talk he had had with Bonardin touching Valgrand, the actor, and Mme. Valgrand, alias — Mme. Raymond.

Juve uttered his reflections aloud.

"This is one riddle the more to solve. I still adhere to the theory that Josephine, some months ago, was brought into intimate relations with Lady Beltham, whose body I discovered at Cité Frochot and later identified."

Fandor sprang up and placed both of his hands upon Juve's shoulders.

"Lady Beltham is not dead: She is alive! As surely as my name's Fandor, the Superior of the Convent at Nogent is — Lady Beltham."

XXVIII
AN OLD PARALYTIC

At the far end of the Rue de Rome Fandor halted. "After all," he thought, "maybe I am going straight into a trap. Who sent me the letter? Who is this M. Mahon? I never heard of him. Why this menacing phrase, 'Come, if you take any interest in the affairs of Lady B —— and F —— .' Oh, if only I could take counsel of Juve!"

But for the last fortnight, since the ill-starred affair of Nogent and the almost incredible discovery he had made that Lady Beltham was still alive, Fandor had not seen Juve. He had been to the Sûreté a number of times, but Juve had vanished.

Fandor stopped before a private house on the Boulevard Pereire North. He passed in through the outer hall and reached the porter's lodge.

"Madame, have you a tenant here named Mahon?"

The porteress came forward.

"M. Mahon? To be sure — fifth floor on the right."

"Thank you. I should like to ask a few questions about him. I have come — to negotiate an insurance policy for him and I should like to know about the value of the furniture in his rooms. What sort of a man is this M. Mahon? About how old is he?"

Fandor had, by pure professional instinct, found the best device in the world. There is not a porteress who has not many times enlightened insurance agents.

"Why, sir, M. Mahon has lived here only a month or six weeks. He can scarcely be very well off, for when he moved in I did not see any fine furniture go up. I believe for that matter he is an old cavalry officer, and, in the army nowadays, folks scarcely make fortunes."

"That's true enough," assented Fandor.

"Anyhow he is a very charming man, an ideal lodger. To begin with, he is infirm, almost paralysed in both legs. I believe he never goes out of an evening. And then he never has any visitors except two young fellows who are serving their time in the army."

"Are they with him now?"

"No, sir, they never come till three or four in the afternoon."

Fandor slipped a coin into the woman's hand and went upstairs. He rang at the door and was surprised at a strange, soft rolling sound.

"Oh, I know," he thought; "the poor man must move about his rooms in a rubber-tired wheel chair."

He was not mistaken. Scarcely was the door opened when he caught sight of an old man of much distinction seated in a wheel chair. This invalid greeted the journalist pleasantly.

"M. Fandor?"

"The same, sir."

M. Mahon pushed forward his chair and motioned to his visitor to come in.

Fandor entered a room in which the curtains were closely drawn and which was brilliantly illuminated with electric lights, although it was the middle of the afternoon. Was it a trap? The journalist instinctively hesitated in the doorway. But behind him a cordial voice called:

"Come in, you all kinds of an idiot!"

The door clicked behind him and the invalid, getting out of his chair, burst into a fit of laughter.

"Juve! Juve!"

"As you see!"

"Bah, what farce are you playing here? Why this lit-up room?"

"All for very good reasons. If you will be kind enough to take a seat, I will explain."

Fandor dropped into a chair staring at Juve, who continued:

"When you came back the other day and told me that unlikely yarn about Lady Beltham being alive, I decided to try new methods. First of all, I became a cavalry officer, then I got this wheel chair and moved into this apartment."

As Juve paused, Fandor, more and more amazed, inquired:

"But your reason for all this!"

"Just wait! The day after the Dixon business, I put three of my best men on the track of the American. I had a notion he would want to see Josephine again, and I was not mistaken. She came back to justify herself in his eyes. The story ended as might have been foreseen. Michel, who brought me the news, said that Josephine had agreed to become Dixon's mistress."

"The deuce!"

"Oh, there is nothing to be surprised at that. Michel made arrangements to learn all the details. Josephine is to live at 33 C in Boulevard Pereire South; that is, to the right of the railway line, fourth floor. Here we are at 24 B Boulevard Pereire North, to left of the railway, fifth floor, and just opposite."

"And what does this old M. Mahon do, Juve?"

Juve smiled.

"You are going to see, my lad."

He settled himself again in the wheel chair, drew a heavy rug over his knees and became once more the old invalid.

"My dear friend, will you open the door for me?"

Fandor laughingly complied, and Juve wheeled himself into another room.

"You see I have plenty of air here thanks to this balcony upon which I can wheel my chair. Would you be good enough to pass me that spy-glass?"

Juve pointed the glass toward the far end of Boulevard Pereire, in the direction of Poste Maillot.

"Mlle. Josephine has lately had a craze for keeping her nails polished."

"But you are not looking toward the house opposite, you are looking in a contrary direction!"

Juve laid his spy-glass on his knees and laughed.

"I expected you to make that remark. See, those glasses at the end are only for show, inside is a whole system of prisms. With this perspective you see not in front of you, but on one side. In other words, when I point it at the far end of the boulevard, what I am really looking at is the house opposite."

Fandor was about to congratulate his friend on this new specimen of his ingenuity, but Juve did not give him time. He startled the journalist by suddenly asking him:

"Tell me, do you love the army?"

"Why?"

"Because I think those two soldiers you see over there are coming."

"To see you," added Fandor.

"How do you know?"

"From your porteress."

"You pumped her?"

"I did. I got her to talk a bit about that excellent M. Mahon."

Juve laughed:

"Confound you!"

With a quick movement Fandor, at the detective's request, drew back the wheel chair and shut the window.

"You understand," explained Juve, "there is nothing to surprise my neighbours in my having two soldiers to visit me. But I don't care for third persons to hear what they say to me." There was a ring at the apartment door. "Go and open, Fandor. I don't leave my cripple's chair for them; people can see through the curtains."

Shown in by Fandor, the soldiers shook hands with Juve and took seats opposite him.

"Do you recognise Michel and Léon?"

"Oh, perfectly!" cried Fandor, "but why this disguise?"

"Because no heed is paid to uniforms, there are soldiers everywhere, and also it is not easy to recognise a civilian suddenly appearing in uniform. What is fresh, Michel?"

"Something pretty serious, sir. According to your instructions we have been shadowing the Superior of the Nogent Convent."

"Well, what have you discovered?"

"Every Tuesday evening the Superior leaves Nogent and goes to Paris."

"Where?"

"To one of the branches of her religious house in the Boulevard Jourdan."

"No. 180?"

Michel was dumbfounded.

"Yes, sir, you knew?"

"No," said Juve, coldly. "What does she do at this branch?"

"There are four or five old nuns there. The Superior spends Tuesday night there and on Wednesday goes back to Nogent about one in the afternoon."

"And you know no more than that?"

"No, sir. Must we go on with the shadowing?"

"No, it is not worth while. Return to the Prefecture and report to M. Havard."

When the two men had left, Fandor turned to Juve.

"What do you make of it?"

Juve shrugged his shoulders.

"Michel is an idiot. That house has two exits; one to the Boulevard, the other to waste ground that leads to the fortifications. The Superior, or Lady Beltham, goes there to change her dress, and then hastens to some prearranged meeting elsewhere. The house at Neuilly will bear watching."

XXIX
THROUGH THE WINDOW

"What a splendid fellow! One can count on him at any time. A friendship like his is rare and precious."

Fandor had just left Juve, and the detective could not help being strangely moved as he thought of the devotion shown him by the journalist.

The detective was still in his wheel chair; with a skilful turn he went back to the balcony and his post of observation.

Evening was coming on. After a fine day the sky had become leaden and overcast with great clouds: a storm was threatening. Juve swore.

"I shan't see much this evening; this confounded Josephine is so sentimental that she loves dreaming in the gloaming at her window without lighting up. Devil take her!"

Juve had armed himself with his spy-glass; he apparently levelled it at Porte Maillot, and in that way he could see something of the movements of Josephine in the rooms opposite him.

"Flowers on the chimney and on the piano! Expecting her lover probably!"

Suddenly he started up in his chair.

"Ah! some one has rung her bell. She is going toward the entrance door."

A minute passed; in the front rooms Juve no longer saw anyone. Josephine must be receiving a visitor.

Some minutes more went by; a heavy shower of rain came down and Juve was forced to leave his balcony.

When he resumed his watching he could not suppress an exclamation of surprise.

"Ah, if he would only turn! This cursed rain prevents me from seeing clearly what is afoot. The brute! Why won't he turn! There, he has laid his bag on a chair, his initials must be on it, but I can't read them. Yet the height of the man! His gestures! It's he, sure enough, it's Chaleck!"

Juve suddenly abandoned his post of observation, propelled his chair to the back room of the suite and seized the telephone apparatus.

"Hello! Give me the Prefecture. It is Juve speaking. Send at once detectives Léon and Michel to No. 33 C Boulevard Pereire South. They are to wait at the door of the house and arrest as they come out the persons I marked as numbers 14 and 15. Let them make haste."

"Assuredly Chaleck won't leave at once if he has come to see Josephine; no doubt he has important things to say. Léon and Michel will arrive in time to nab him first and Josephine after. And to-morrow, when I have them handcuffed before me, it's the deuce if I don't manage to get the truth out of them."

Juve went back to his look-out.

"Oh, they seem very lively, both of them; the talk must be serious. Josephine doesn't look pleased. She seems to disagree with what Chaleck is saying. One would think he was giving her orders. No! she is down on her knees. A declaration of love! After Loupart and Dixon it's that infernal doctor's turn!"

Juve watched for a moment longer the young woman and the mysterious and elusive Chaleck.

"Ah! that's what I feared! Chaleck is going and Léon and Michel haven't come!"

Juve hesitated. Should he go down, rush to the Boulevard and try to collar the ruffian? That wasn't possible. Juve lived on the fifth floor, so that he had one more story to get down than Chaleck, then there was the railway line between him and Josephine's house. Chaleck would have ample time to disappear. But Juve reassured himself.

"Luckily he has left his hold-all, and if I mistake not, that is his stick on the chair. Therefore he expects to come back."

Powerless to act, Juve witnessed the exit of Chaleck, who soon appeared at the door of Josephine's house and went striding off. Juve followed him with his eyes, intensely chagrined. Would he ever again find such a good opportunity of laying hands on the ruffian?

Chaleck vanished round the corner of the street, and Juve again took to watching Josephine! The young woman did not appear to be upset by her late visitor. She sat, her elbows on the table, turning with a listless finger the pages of a volume.

"Clearly he is coming back," thought Juve, "or he would not have left his things there. I shall nab him in a few days at latest."

Juve was about to leave his post of observation when he saw Josephine raise her head in an attitude of listening to an indefinable and mysterious noise.

"What is going on?" Juve asked himself. "She cannot be already watching for Chaleck's return."

Then Juve started.

"Oh! oh!"

He had just seen Josephine at a single bound spring toward the window. The young woman gazed steadily in front of her, her arms outstretched in a posture of horror. She seemed in a state of abject terror. There was no mistaking her motions. She was panic-stricken, panting, trembling in all her limbs. Juve, who lost no movement of the hapless woman, felt a cold sweat break out on his forehead.

"What's the matter with her? There is nobody in the room, I see nothing! What can frighten her to that extent? Oh, my God!"

Forgetting all precautions, all the comedy he was preparing so carefully for the neighbour's benefit, he sprang to his feet, deserting his wheel chair. His hands clenched on the rail of the balcony while spellbound by the sight he beheld, he leaned over the rail as if in a frantic desire to fling himself to the young woman's help. Josephine had bestridden the sash of her window. She was now standing on the ledge, holding with one hand to the rail of her balcony and her body flung backwards as if mad with terror.

"What is happening? Oh, the poor soul!"

Josephine, uttering a desperate cry, had let go of the supporting rail and had flung herself into space. Juve saw the young woman's body spin in the air, heard the dull thud that it made as it crashed against the ground.

"It is monstrous!"

Juve beside himself tore down the stairs full tilt, passed breathlessly the porteress, who seemed likely to faint at the sight of the headlong pace of the supposed paralytic.

He went round Boulevard Pereire, darted along the railway line, and, panting, got to the side of the ill-starred Josephine. At the sound of her fall and the cries she uttered people had flown to the windows, passers-by had turned round: when Juve got there a ring of people had already formed round the unfortunate woman. The detective roughly pushed some of them aside, knelt down beside the body and put his ear to the chest.

"Dead? No!"

A faint groan came from the lips of the poor sufferer. Juve realised that by unheard-of luck, Josephine, in the course of her fall, had struck the outer branches of one of the trees that fringed the Boulevard. This had somewhat broken the shock, but her legs were frightfully broken and one of her arms hung lifeless.

"Quick!" commanded Juve. "A cab; take her to the hospital."

As soon as help was forthcoming, Juve, recalled to the duties of his profession, asked himself:

"What can have occurred? What was it she tried to escape by throwing herself into space? I saw the whole room, there was no one with her. She must have been the victim of a delusion."

XXX
UNCLE AND NEPHEW

"So, uncle, you have decided to live at Neuilly?"

"Oh, it's quite settled. Your aunt finds the place charming, and besides, it would be so pleasant to have a garden. Also, the land is sure to grow more valuable in this neighbourhood and the purchase of a house here would be a good speculation!"

The stout man, as he uttered the word "speculation," beamed. The mere sight of him suggested the small tradesman grown rich by dint of long and arduous years of toil, retired from business and prone to fancy he was a man of genius.

Compared with him the young man he styled nephew, slim, elaborately elegant, his little moustache carefully curled, gave the impression of coming out of a draper's shop and wanting to be taken for a swell. Evidently the nephew courted the uncle and flattered him.

"You are right, land speculations are very sure and very profitable. So you wrote to the caretaker of the house to let you view it?"

"I did, and he answered, 'Come to-day or to-morrow. I shall be at your orders.' That is why I sent you word to go with me, for since you are the sole heir of my fortune — — "

"Oh, uncle, you may be sure — — "

The Madeleine tramway where the two men were talking aloud, heeding little the amused notice of the other passengers, pulled up a moment in the Place de l'Eglise at Neuilly.

"Let us get down. Boulevard Inkermann begins here."

With the pantings and gaspings of a man whose stoutness made all physical exercise irksome, the uncle lowered himself off the footboard of the tram. The young man sprang to his side. After five minutes' walk the two men were in front of Lady Beltham's house, the identical house to which Juve and Fandor had previously come before to make exhaustive inquiries.

"You see, my boy," declared the stout party, "it is not at all a bad looking house. Evidently it has not been lived in for a long time, its state of outside dilapidation shows how neglected it has been, but it is possible that inside there may not be many repairs to be made."

"In any case, the garden is very fine."

"Yes, the grounds are large enough. And then what I like is its wonderful seclusion: the wall surrounding it on all sides is very high, and the entrance gate would be hard for robbers to tackle."

"Shall I ring?"

"Yes, ring."

The young man pressed the button, a peal rang out in the distance: presently the porter appeared. He was a big fellow with long whiskers and a distinguished air, the perfect type of the high-class servant.

"You gentlemen have come to see the house?"

"Exactly. I am M. Durant. It is I who wrote to you."

"To be sure, sir, I remember."

The porter showed the two visitors into the garden, and forthwith the stout man drew his nephew along the paths. The sense of proprietorship came over him at once; he spared his relative none of the points of the property.

"You see, Emile, it isn't big, but still it is amply sufficient. No trees before the house, which allows a view of the Boulevard from all the windows. The servants' quarters being in the far part of the garden can in no way annoy the people in the house: Notice, too, that the trees are quite young and their foliage thin. I don't care for too luxuriant gardens which are apt to block the view."

"That's right, Uncle."

The porter, who was following the two, broke in upon the ecstasy of the prospective owner.

"Would you gentlemen like to see the house?"

"Why, certainly, certainly."

The stout man, however, before entering, was bent on going round it. He noticed the smallest details, growing more and more enthusiastic.

"Look, Emile, it is very well built. The ground floor is sufficiently raised so as not to be too damp. This big terrace, on which the three French windows open, must be very cheerful in summer. Oh, there are drain pipes at the four corners! And we mustn't fail to see the cellars. I'm sure they are very fine. Bend down over the air-holes; what do you think of the gratings that close them? And, now, shall we go in?"

The porter led them to the main entrance door.

"Here is the vestibule, gentlemen, to the left, the servants' hall and kitchen; to the right, the dining-room; facing you a small drawing-room, then the large drawing-room, and, lastly, the double staircase leading to the first floor."

The stout man dropped into a chair.

"And to whom does this place belong?"

"Lady Beltham, sir."

"She does not live here?"

"Not now. At this moment she is travelling."

In the wake of the porter, uncle and nephew went through the rooms on the ground floor. As happens in all untenanted houses, the damp had wrought terrible havoc. The flooring, worm-eaten, creaked under their feet, the carpets had large damp spots on them, the paper hung loose on the walls, while the furniture was covered with a thick coat of dust.

"Don't pay any attention to the furniture, Emile, it matters little; what we must first look at is the arrangement of the rooms. Why, there are iron shutters — I like that."

"To be sure, Uncle, they are very practical."

"Yes, yes; to begin with, when those shutters are closed it would be impossible from the outside to see anything in the rooms. Not even the least light."

The porter proceeded to show them the first floor of the house.

"There is only one staircase?" asked the stout man.

"Yes, only one."

"And what is the cause of the unusual dampness? We are far from the Seine; the garden is not very leafy."

"There is a leaky cistern in the cellars, sir. Here is the largest bedroom. It was my Lady's."

"Yes, one sees it has been the last room to be lived in."

At this harmless remark the porter seemed very upset.

"What makes you think that, sir?"

"Why, the chairs are pushed about as though recently used. There is much less dust on the furniture. And — there's a print — look at the desk, there is a trace of dust on the diary. The blotting paper has been moved lately, some one has been writing there — why, what's wrong with you?"

As he listened to the stout man's remarks the porter grew strangely pale.

"Oh," he stammered, "it's nothing, nothing at all."

"One would say you were afraid."

"Afraid? No, sir. I am not afraid — only — — "

"Only what?"

"Well, gentlemen, it is best not to stay here — Lady Beltham is selling the house because it is — haunted!"

Neither of the visitors seemed impressed by the statement of their guide. The elder laughed a jolly laugh.

"Are there ghosts?"

"Why, sir, 'spirits' come here."

"Have you seen them?"

"Oh! certainly not, sir. When they are there, I shut myself up in the lodge, I can assure you — — "

"When do they appear?"

"They come almost always on Tuesday nights."

And warming to his subject the porter gave details. He got the impression first on one occasion when her Ladyship was absent. She had left some days before for Italy. It was Sunday, and then during Tuesday night while walking in the garden he heard movements inside the house.

"I went to fetch my keys and when I came back I found nobody! I thought at first it was burglars, but I saw nothing had been taken away. Yet, I was not mistaken, furniture had been moved. There were bread crumbs on the floor."

The young man roared with laughter.

"Bread crumbs! Then your spirits come and sup here?"

The uncle, equally amused, asked:

"And what did Lady Beltham think when you told her that?"

"Lady Beltham laughed at me. But, sir, I had my own ideas. I watched in the garden daily and I heard the same sounds and always on Tuesday nights. At last I laid a trap; I put a chalk mark round the chairs in Lady Beltham's room, she being still away. Well, sir, when I came to the house again on Thursday the chairs had been moved. I told Lady Beltham, and this time she seemed very much frightened. It is since then she made up her mind to sell the house."

"For all that, what makes you say they are spirits?"

"What else could it be, sir. I also heard the sounds of chains jangling. One night I even heard a strange and terrible hiss."

"Well!" cried the stout man, beginning to go down the staircase, "since the house is haunted I shall have to pay less for it; eh, Emile?"

"You will buy, sir, in spite of that?"

"To be sure. Your phantoms alarm me less than the damp."

"Oh, the damp? That can be easily remedied. You will see that we have a central heating stove installed."

The porter led his visitors down a narrow stair to the cellars.

"Take care, gentlemen, the stairs are slippery."

Then he observed: "You don't need a candle, the gratings are big enough to give plenty of light."

"What is that?" asked the young man, pointing to a huge iron cylinder embedded in the earth and rising some four-and-a-half feet above the floor.

"The cistern of which I spoke, as you can see for yourselves, it is all but full."

The porter hurried them on.

"That is the heating stove. There are conductors throughout the house. When it is in full blast the house is even too warm."

"But your grate stove is in pieces!" objected the stout man, pointing with his stick to iron plates torn out of one side of the central furnace.

"Oh, sir, that happened at the time of the floods. But it won't cost much to put it right. If you gentlemen will examine the inside of the apparatus you will see that the pipes are in perfect order."

The uncle followed the porter's suggestion.

"Your pipes are as big as chimneys; a man could pass through them."

The inspection ended, uncle and nephew bestowed a liberal tip on their guide. They would think it over and write or come again soon.

The two relatives retraced their steps to Boulevard Inkermann.

"Fandor?"

"Juve?"

"We have got them!"

Uncle and nephew — that is to say, Juve and Fandor — could talk quite freely now.

"Juve, are you certain that we have got them?"

Juve pushed his friend into a wine-shop and ordered drinks. He then drew from his pocket a piece of paper, quite blank.

"What is that?"

"A bit of paper I picked up on Lady Beltham's desk while the porter's back was turned. It will serve for a little experiment. If it is not long since a hand rested on it, we shall find the print."

"On this blank paper?"

"Yes, Fandor. Look!"

Juve drew a pencil from his pocket and scratched off a fine dust of graphite which he shook over the paper. Gradually the outline of a hand appeared, faint, but quite visible.

"That is how," resumed Juve, "with this very simple process, you can decipher the finger prints of persons who have written or rested their hands on anything — paper, glass, even wood. According to the clearness of this outline which is thrown up by the coagulation of the plumbago — thanks to the ordinary moisture of the hand — which was laid on the paper, I can assure you that some one wrote on Lady Beltham's desk about ten days ago."

"It is wonderful," said Fandor. "Here, then, is proof positive that her Ladyship visits her house from time to time."

"Correct — or at least that some one goes there, for that is a man's hand."

"Well, what are you going to do now, Juve?"

"Now? I'm off to the Prefecture to get rid of my false embonpoint, which bothers me no end. I have never been so glad that I am not naturally stout."

Fandor laughed.

"And I own to you that I shan't be sorry to get rid of my false moustache. All the while I was inspecting that cursed house, this moustache kept tickling my nose and making me want to sneeze."

"You should have done so."

"But suppose my moustache had come off?"

XXXI
LOVERS AND ACCOMPLICES

"Oh! who is that?"

From the shadow issued some one who calmly replied:

"It is I."

"Ah! — I know you now, but why this disguise?"

"Madame the Superior — I present myself — Doctor Chaleck. Isn't my disguise as good as yours?"

"What do you want of me? Speak quickly, I am frightened."

"To begin with, I thank you for coming to the tryst at your house — at ours. For five Tuesdays I have waited in vain. But first, madame, explain your sudden conversion, the reason of your sudden entry into Orders. That is a strange device for the mistress of Gurn."

Doctor Chaleck held under the lash of his irony the unhappy woman who seemed overcome by anxiety. The two were facing each other in the large room that formed the middle of the first floor of the house in Boulevard Inkermann at Neuilly. It was, in fact, the only room fit to use: they had left to neglect and inclement weather the other rooms in the elegant mansion which some years before was considered in the Parisian world as one of the most comfortable and luxurious in the foreign colony.

It was in truth here that in days gone by the tragic drama had been played: death had laid its cold hand upon the gilded trappings of the great apartment and laughter and joy had taken flight. However, time passes so quickly and evil memories so soon grow dim that many had forgotten the grim happenings which three years before had beset the mansion on the Boulevard.

It was at first the deep mourning of Lady Beltham whose husband had been mysteriously done to death at Belleville. Then, some weeks later, occurred the awful scene of the arrest of Lord Beltham's murderer, just as he was leaving the house, an arrest due to Juve, who, though he succeeded in laying hands on the assassin, the infamous Gurn, was not able to prove — sure though he might be of it — that the slayer of the husband was the lover of the wife.

After these shocking events Lady Beltham left France, dismissing the many attendants with whom she loved to surround herself like a true queen of beauty, luxury and wealth.

At rare intervals the Lady, whose existence grew more and more mysterious, went back for a few days to her house at Neuilly. She would vanish, would reappear, living like a recluse, almost in entire solitude, receiving none of her old acquaintances.

About a year ago she seemed to want to settle finally at Boulevard Inkermann. Workmen began to put the house in order again, the lodge was opened and a family of caretakers came; then suddenly the work had been broken off; some weeks went by while Lady Beltham lived alone with her companion; then both disappeared.

Lady Beltham shivered, and, gathering about her shoulders the cloak which covered her religious habit, muttered: "I'm cold."

"Beastly weather, and to think this is July."

Chaleck crossed to a register in the corner of the room.

"No good to leave that open! An icy wind comes through the passage to the cellar."

Lady Beltham turned in alarm toward her enigmatic companion.

"Why did you let it be supposed I was dead?"

"Why did you yourself leave here two days before the crime at the Cité Frochot?"

Lady Beltham hung her head and with a sob in her voice:

"I was deserted and jealous. Besides, I was enduring frightful remorse. The idea had come to me to write down the terrible secret which haunted my spirit, to give the story to some one I could trust, an attorney, and then — — "

"Go on, pray!"

"And, then, what I had written suddenly vanished. It was after that I lost my head and fled. I had long been meaning to withdraw from the world. The Sisters of St. Clotilde offered to receive me in their house at Nogent."

Chaleck added brutally:

"That isn't all. You forgot to say you were afraid. Come, be frank, afraid of Gurn, of me!"

"Well, yes, I was afraid, not so much of you, but of our crimes. I am also afraid of dying."

"That confession you wrote became known to some one who confided it to me."

"Heavens," murmured the unhappy woman. "Who mentioned it?"

Chaleck had again crossed to the register, which, although closed by him some moments before, was open again, letting into the room a blast of icy air from the basement.

"This can't stay shut, it must be seen to," he muttered.

Lady Beltham, shaken by a nervous tremour, insisted:

"Who betrayed me? Who told?"

Chaleck seated himself by her side.

"You remember Valgrand, the actor? Well, Valgrand was married. His wife sought to clear up the mystery of his disappearance and went — where, I ask you? Why, to you, Lady Beltham! You took her as companion! It would have been impossible to introduce a more redoubtable spy into the house than the widow Valgrand, known by you under the false name of Mme. Raymond."

Lady Beltham remained panic-stricken.

"We are lost!"

Chaleck squeezed her two hands in a genuine burst of affection.

"We are saved!" he shouted. "Mme. Raymond will talk no more!"

"The body at the Cité Frochot!"

Chaleck nodded. "Yes."

She looked at him in alarm, mingled with repulsion and horror.

"Now, understand that that death saved you, and if I saved you it is because I loved you, love you still, will always love you!"

Lady Beltham, overcome, let herself fall into Chaleck's arms, her head resting on her lover's shoulder as she wept hot tears.

Lady Beltham was once more enslaved, a captive! More than two years ago she had broken with the mysterious and terrible being whom she had once egged on to kill her husband, and with whom she then committed the most appalling of crimes. During this separation the unhappy woman had tried to pull herself together, to acquire a fresh honesty of mind and body, a new soul; dreamed of finding again in religion some help, some forgetfulness. She had later experienced the frightful tortures of jealousy, knowing her late lover had mistresses! But she resisted the craving to see him again, and pictured him to herself in such terrible guise that she felt an overwhelming fear of finding herself face to face with him. Now the season of calm and quiet she had evoked was suddenly dispelled. First came the mysterious disappearance of her confession and the weird crime of the Cité Frochot following on its loss. To be sure she did not then know that Doctor Chaleck, of whom the papers spoke, was none other than Gurn, but had they not in *La Capitale* spoken of Fantômas in that connection? And at this disquieting comparison Lady Beltham had felt sinister forebodings. Other mysteries had then supervened, unaccountable to the guilty lady who by that time was already seeking her new birth in the bosom of Religion. Alas! her miseries were to grow definite enough.

At the very gate of the convent an innocent man, Bonardin, the actor, fell victim to the attack of Juve, also innocent, and in that affair she felt the complicity of her late lover grow more and more certain. She then received a letter from him, followed by a second. Gurn called her to his place — their place — the mansion at Neuilly, every Tuesday night. She held out several times despite threatened reprisals. At last she yielded and went: she expected Gurn — it was Chaleck she found. The two were one!

From henceforth she was faced with this accomplice, guilty of new crimes, clothed in a new personality, already under suspicion, which doubtless he would cast off only to assume another which would enable him still further to extend the list of his crimes! But despite all the horror her lover inspired her with she felt herself tamed again, powerless to resist him, ready to do anything the moment he bade her!

She inquired feebly:

"Who was it killed Mme. Raymond? Was it that ruffian — whom they speak of in the papers — Loupart?"

"Well, not exactly!"

"Then was it you? Speak, I would rather know."

"It was neither he nor I, and yet it was to some extent both."

"I do not understand."

"It is rather difficult to understand. Our 'executioner' does not lack originality. I may say it is something which lives yet does not think."

"Who is it! Who is it!"

"Why not ask Detective Juve. Oh! Juve, too, would like to know who the deuce all these people are. Gurn, Chaleck, Loupart, and, above all — Fantômas!"

"Fantômas! Ah, I scarcely dare utter that name. And yet a doubt oppresses my heart! Tell me, are you not, yourself — Fantômas?"

Chaleck freed himself gently, for Lady Beltham had wound her arms round his neck.

"I know nothing, I am merely the lover who loves you."

"Then let us go far away. Let us begin a new existence together. Will you? Come!" She stopped all at once — "I heard a noise." Chaleck, too, listened. Some slight creakings had, indeed, disturbed the hush of the room. But outside the wind and the rain whirled around the dilapidated, lonely abode, and it was not surprising that unaccountable sounds should be audible in the stillness. Once more Lady Beltham built up her plans, catching a glimpse of a future all peace and happiness.

With a brief, harsh remark, Chaleck brought her back to reality.

"All that cannot be, at least for the moment, we must first — — "

Lady Beltham laid her hand on his lips.

"Do not speak!" she begged. "A fresh crime — that's what you mean?"

"A vengeance, an execution! A man has set himself to run me down, has determined my ruin: between us it is a struggle without quarter; my life is not safe but at the cost of his, so he must perish. In four days they will find Detective Juve dead in his own bed. And with him will finally vanish the fiction he has evoked of Fantômas! Fantômas! Ah, if society knew — if humanity, instead of being what it is — but it matters little!"

"And Fantômas? What will become of him — of you?"

"Have I told you that I was Fantômas?"

"No," stammered she, "but — — "

The dim light of a pale dawn filtered through the closed shutters of the big drawing-room in which lover and mistress had met again, after long weeks of separation, to call up sinister memories. For all their hopes the limit of the tribulations to which they were a prey seemed still far off.

Chaleck blew out the lamp. He drew aside the curtains. Sharply he put an end to the interview:

"I am off, Lady Beltham. Soon we shall meet again. Never let anyone suspect what we have said to each other — Farewell."

The hapless woman, crushed and broken by emotion, remained nearly an hour alone in the great room. Then the requirements of her official life came to her mind. It was necessary to return to the convent at Nogent.

Extricating themselves painfully from the pipes of the great stove, Juve and Fandor, covered with plaster, wreathed with cobwebs, and freely sprinkled with dust, fell back suddenly into the middle of the cellar. The two men, heedless of the disarray of their dress and their painful cramped limbs, spoke both at once, dumbfounded but joyful:

"Well, Juve?"

"Well, Fandor, we got something for our money."

"Oh, what a lovely night, Juve; I wouldn't have given up my place for a fortune."

"We had front seats, though to be sure the velvet armchairs were lacking."

They were silent for a moment, their minds fully occupied with a crowd of ideas. So Chaleck and Loupart were one and the same? And Lady Beltham was indeed the accomplice of Gurn. An unhappy accomplice, repentant, wretched, a criminal through love.

"Fandor, they are ours now. Let us act!"

The pair, not sorry to breathe a little more easily than they had done for the past few hours, went upstairs, reached the ground floor and made their way into the drawing-room, where during the night Doctor Chaleck and Lady Beltham had had their memorable interview.

Juve, without a word, paced up and down the room, poking in all the corners, then gave a cry:

"Here is the famous mouth of the heater which that brute Chaleck tried to shut, and I persisted in opening so as not to lose a word of his instructive conversation. No matter, if he felt cold, what did I feel like?"

"The fact is," added Fandor, whose hoarse voice bore witness to the difficulties he had just passed through, "these stove pipes have very little comfort about them."

"What can you expect?" cried Juve. "The architect did not think of us when he built the house. And now, Fandor, we have a hard task before us and we need all the luck we can get. For certainly it is Fantômas we have unearthed: Fantômas, the lover of Lady Beltham, the slayer of her husband, the murderer of Valgrand, the master that got rid of Mme. Raymond! Gurn, Chaleck, Loupart. The one being who can be all those and himself too — Fantômas."

As the two friends left Lady Beltham's house without attracting notice, the detective drew from his pocket a species of little scale which he showed Fandor.

"What do you make of that?"

"I haven't the least idea."

"Well, I have, and it may put us in the way of a great discovery. Did you notice that Chaleck did not say definitely who the 'executioner' of Mme. Raymond was?"

"To be sure."

"Well, I believe that I have a morsel of this 'executioner' in my pocket."

XXXII

THE SILENT EXECUTIONER

Juve was in his study smoking a cigarette. It was nine in the evening. The door leading to the lobby opened and Fandor walked in.

"All right, this evening?"

"All right. What brings you here, Fandor?"

The journalist smiled and pointed to a calendar on the wall: "The fact that — it's this evening, Juve."

"The date fixed by Chaleck or Fantômas for my demise. To-morrow morning I am to be found in my bed, strangled, crushed, or something of the sort. I suppose you've come to get a farewell interview for *La Capitale*. To gather the minutest details of the frightful crime so that you can publish a special edition. '*The tragedy in Rue Bonaparte! Juve overcome by Fantômas!*'"

Fandor listened, amused at the detective's outburst.

"You'd be angry with me, Juve," he declared, in the same jocular strain, "for passing by such a sensational piece of news, wouldn't you?"

"That is so. And then I own I expected my last evening to be a lonely one, there was a feeling of sadness at the bottom of my heart. I thought that before dying I should have liked to say farewell to young Fandor, whose life I am continually putting in peril by my crazy ventures, but whom I love as the surest of companions, the sagest of advisers, the most discreet of confidants."

Fandor was touched. With a spontaneous movement he sprang to the armchair in which Juve sat, seized and wrung the detective's hands.

"What?"

"I shall stay here. You don't suppose I'm going to leave you to pass this night alone?"

Juve, touched beyond measure by Fandor's words, seemed uncertain what he ought to decide.

"I can't pretend, Fandor, that your presence is not agreeable, and I'm grateful to you for your sympathy; I knew I could count on you: but after all, lad, we must look ahead and consider all contingencies. Fantômas may succeed! Now you know what I have set out to do; if I should fail, I should like to think that you would carry on the work as my successor and put an end to Fantômas."

"But, Juve, you are threatened by Fantômas; that is why I am here to help you."

"Well, I have no bed to put you in."

Fandor, taken aback, stared at the detective. The latter rose and began walking about the room, then turned sharply and gazed at the young man:

"You are quite determined to stay with me?"

"Yes."

"And if I bade you go?"

"I should disobey you."

"Very well, then," concluded Juve, shrugging his shoulders, "come along and light me."

The detective passed out of the apartment and made for the stairs.

"Where are we bound for?" asked Fandor.

"The garret," Juve replied.

A quarter of an hour later Juve and Fandor dragged into the bedroom a huge open-work wicker-basket.

"Whew!" cried Juve, mopping his forehead, "no one would believe it was so heavy."

Fandor smiled.

"It's full of rubbish. Really, Juve, you are not a tidy man!"

Juve, without reply, proceeded to empty the basket, pulling out books, linen, pieces of wood, carpet, rolls of paper; in fact, the accumulated refuse of fifteen years.

"What is your height?" he asked.

"If I remember right, five feet ten."

Juve got out his pocket measure and took the length of the crate.

"That's all right," he murmured. "You'll be quite snug and comfortable in it."

Fandor burst out:

"You're a cheerful host, Juve. You bottle up your guests in cages now!"

Juve placed a mattress at the bottom of the basket and laid two blankets over that, then he put a pillow on top. Patting the bedding to make it smooth, he declared with a laugh:

"I fear nothing, but I have taken precautions. I have posted two men in the porter's lodge. I have loaded my revolver, and dined comfortably. About half-past eleven I shall go to bed as usual. However, instead of going to sleep I shall endeavour to keep awake. At dinner I took three cups of coffee, and when you go I shall drink a fourth."

"Excuse me," said Fandor, "but I am not going away."

"There! You'll sleep splendid inside that, Fandor."

The journalist, used to the devices of his friend, nodded his head. Juve had already taken off his coat and waistcoat and now drew from a box three belts half a yard in breadth and studded outside with sharp points. "Look, Fandor! I shall be completely protected when I am swathed in them. Oh," he added, "I was going to forget my leg guards!"

Juve went back to the box and took out two other rolls, also studded with spikes. Fandor looked in amazement at this gear and Juve observed laughingly:

"It will cost me a pair of sheets and maybe a mattress."

"What does it mean?"

"These defensive works have a double object. To protect me against Fantômas, or the 'executioner' he will send, and also I shall be able to determine the civil status of the 'executioner' in question."

Fandor, more and more puzzled, inspected the iron spikes, which were two or more inches in length.

"This contrivance is not new," said Juve; "Liabeuf wore arm guards like these under his jacket, and when the officers wanted to seize him they tore their hands."

"I know, I know," replied Fandor, "but —— "

The detective all at once laid a finger on his lips.

"It's now twenty past eleven, and I am in the habit of being in bed at half past. Fantômas is bound to know it: when he comes or sends, he must not notice anything out of the way. Get into your wicker case and shut the lid down carefully. By the by, I shall leave the window slightly open."

"Isn't that a bit risky?"

"It is one of my habits, and not to make Fantômas suspicious I alter my ways in nothing."

Fandor settled himself in his case and Juve also got into bed. As he put out the light he gave a warning.

"We mustn't close an eye or utter a word. Whatever happens, don't move. But when I call, strike a light at once and come to me."

"All right," replied Fandor.

"Fandor!"

Juve's cry rent the stillness of the night, loud and compelling. The journalist leaped from his wicker-basket so abruptly that he knocked against the lamp stand and the lamp fell to the floor. Fandor searched for his matches in vain.

"Light up, Fandor!" shouted Juve.

The noise of a struggle, the dull thud of a fall on the floor, maddened the journalist. In the darkness he heard Juve groaning, scraping the floor with his boots, making violent efforts to resist some mysterious assailant.

"Be quick, in God's name," implored the pain-wrung voice of the detective. Fandor trod on the glass of the lamp, which broke. He tripped, knocked his head against a press, rebounded, then suddenly uttered a terrible cry. His hands, outstretched apart, in the gloom, had brushed a cold, shiny body which slid under his palms.

"Fandor! Help, Fandor!"

Desperate, Fandor plunged haphazard about the disordered chamber, wrapped in darkness. Suddenly, he rushed into the study hard by, found there another lamp which he lit in haste, and hurried back with it.

A fearful sight wrung a cry of terror from him. Juve, on his knees on the floor, was covered with blood.

"Juve!"

"It's all right, Fandor. Some one has bled, but not I."

The detective rushed to the open window and leaned out into the dark night.

"Listen!" he cried. "Do you hear that low hissing, that dull rustling?"

"Yes. I heard it just now."

"It was the 'executioner.'"

The detective drew back into the room, shut the window, pulled down the blinds, and then took off his armour. Curiously he examined the stains of blood, the tiny shreds of flesh that had remained on the points.

"We have no more to fear now," he said, "the stroke has been tried — and has failed."

"Juve! tell me what has just happened? I may be an idiot, but I don't understand at all!"

"You are no fool, Fandor; far from it, but if in many circumstances you reason and argue with considerable aptness, I grant you far less deductive faculty. That does not seem to be your forte."

Fandor seated himself before the detective, and the latter held forth.

"When we found ourselves faced with the first crime, that of the Cité Frochot, and our notice was drawn to the elusive Fantômas, we were unable to decide in what manner that hapless Mme. Raymond, whom we then took for Lady Beltham, had been done to death. Now, remember, Fandor, that during that night of mystery, hidden behind the curtains in Chaleck's study we heard weird rustlings and faint sort of hissings, didn't we?"

"We did," admitted Fandor, at a loss, "but go on, Juve."

"When we were called to investigate the attack on the American, Dixon, it was easy for us to conclude that the attempt of which the pugilist had been the object was the outcome of the same plan of battle as that which cost the widow Valgrand her life. The mysterious 'executioner,' which Chaleck did not disguise from Lady Beltham, was thus a being endowed with vigour enough to completely crush a woman's body, and likely do as much to that of an ordinary man. But the 'executioner' in question was not strong enough to get the better of the grand physique of the champion pugilist, since it failed in its attempt.

"This instrument 'of limited power,' if I may so describe it, must then be, not a mechanism which nothing can resist, but a living being! It must also be a creature striking panic, terrifying, formidable: you ask why, Fandor?"

"Yes, to be sure."

"I am going to tell you. If our poor friend Josephine were not still in a high fever she would certainly uphold me. You remember the business on the Boulevard Pereire? Chaleck or Fantômas wants to be rid of the woman he loved under the guise of Loupart, since he has gone back to Lady Beltham. Moreover, Josephine chatters too much with Dixon, with the police.

"Chaleck, Fantômas, therefore, goes up to Josephine's. After having told the poor creature I know not what yarn, he departs, leaving behind in his hold-all, the instrument. Now this last, when it shows itself, so terrifies the poor girl that she throws herself out of the window."

"I begin to see what you mean," said the journalist.

"Listen," replied Juve. "The mysterious, nameless and terrible accomplice of Fantômas, is no other than a snake! A snake trained to crush bodies in its coils. After having long suspected its existence, I began to be sure of it when I found that strange scale at Neuilly. This accounts for the incomprehensible state of Mme. Valgrand's body, the extraordinary attempt on Dixon, the murderous thing that terrified Josephine! That is why, expecting to-night's visit, I barbed myself with iron like a knight of old, feeling pretty sure that if the hands of the officers were torn by the armlets of Liabeuf, the coils of Fantômas' serpent would be flayed on touching my sharp spikes."

"Juve!" cried Fandor, "if I hadn't had the bad luck to upset the lamp, we should have caught this frightful beast."

"Probably, but what should we have done with it? After all, it's better that it should go back to Fantômas."

"But you haven't yet told me what happened!"

The young man's face displayed such curiosity that Juve burst out laughing.

"Journalist! Incorrigible newsmonger! All right, take notes for your article describing this appalling adventure. So, then, Fandor, the lamp once out, the hours go by, a trifle more slowly in the darkness than in the light. You are silent and still like a little Moses in your wicker cradle. As for me, armoured as I was, I tried not to stir in my bed — to spare the sheets — Juve is not wealthy. Midnight, one o'clock, two, the quarter past. How long it is! — Then, an alarm! A cat that mews strangely. Then comes that little hissing sound I begin to know. Hiss — hiss! Oh, what a horrid feeling! I guess that the window is opening wider. You heard, as I did, Fandor, the revolting scales grit on the boards. But you didn't know what it was, whereas I did know it was the snake! I swear to you it needed all my pluck not to flinch, for I wanted at any cost to see it through to the end, and know whether, behind this reptile, Fantômas was not going to show his vile snout.

"Ah, the brute, how quickly he went to work. As I was listening, my muscles tense, my nerves on edge, I suddenly felt my sheet stir — the foul beast is trained to attack beds, remember the attack on Dixon — and suddenly it was the grip, furious, quick as a whip stroke, twining about me. I was thrown down, tossed, shaken, torn like a feather, tied up like a sausage!

"My arms glued to my body, my loins hampered. I intended not to say a word, I had faith in my iron-work; but to be frank, I was scared, awfully scared. And I yelled: 'Fandor! Help!'

"Oh, those accursed moments. He began to squeeze horribly when all at once I felt a cold liquid flow over my skin — blood. The brute was wounded. We still wrestled, and you tripped in the darkness and smashed the glass of the lamp, and I was choking gradually. All my life I shall remember it. And then, what relief, what joy when the grip slackened, when he gives up and makes off. The beast glided over the floor, reached the window, hissed frantically and vanished. There, M. Reporter, you have impressions from life, and rough ones, too! Well, the luck is turning, and I think it is veering to our quarter. Things are going from bad to worse for Fantômas. I tell you, Fandor, we shall nab him before long!"

XXXIII

A SCANDAL IN THE CLOISTER

Slight sounds, scarcely audible, disturbed the peace of the cloister. In the absolute silence of the night, vague noises could be distinguished. Furtive steps, whisperings, doors opened or shut cautiously. Then the blinking light of a candle shone at a casement, two or three other windows were illuminated and the hubbub grew general. Voices were heard, frightened interjections, the stir increased in the long corridor on which cells opened. Generally the curtains of these cells were discreetly drawn; now they were being pulled aside. Drowsy faces looked out of the gloom; the excitement increased.

"Sister Marguerite! Sister Vincent! Sister Clotilde! What is it? What is happening? Listen!"

The alarmed nuns gathered at the far end of the passage. The worthy women, roused from their rest, had hastily arranged their coifs, and chastely wrapped themselves in their flowing robes. They turned their frightened faces toward the chapel.

"Burglars!" murmured the Sister who was treasurer of the convent, thinking of the cup of gold that the humble little sisterhood preserved as a relic with jealous care.

Another Sister, recently come from the creuse, from which she had been driven by the laws, did not conceal her fears.

"More emissaries of the government! They are going to turn us out!"

The Senior, Sister Vincent, quivering with alarm, stammered:

"It is a revolution — I saw that in '70."

A heap of chairs under the vaulting suddenly toppled down. Panic stricken, the sisters crowded closed together, not daring to go to the chapel, which was joined to the passage by a little staircase.

"And the Mother Superior, what did she think of it all — what would she say?"

They drew near the cell, a little apart from the others, occupied by the lady, who, on taking the headship of the "House," had brought with her precious personal assistance and a good deal of money as well. Sister Vincent, who had gone forward and was about to enter the little chamber, drew back.

"Our Holy Mother," she informed the others, "is at her prayers."

At this very moment broken cries rang down the passage. Sister Frances, the janitress, who everyone believed was calmly slumbering in her lodge, suddenly appeared, her eyes wild, her garments in disarray.

The sisters gathered round her, but the helpless woman shrieked, quite beside herself.

"Let me go! Let us flee! I have seen the devil! He is there! In the church! It is frightful!"

Mad with terror, the Sister explained in disjointed phrases what had alarmed her. She had heard a noise and fancied it might be the gardener's dog shut by mistake in the chapel. Then behold! At the moment she entered the choir the stained-glass window above the shrine of St. Clotilde, their patroness, suddenly gave way, and through the opening appeared a supernatural being who came toward her ejaculating words she could not understand. Armed with a great cudgel, he struck right and left, making a terrible uproar.

Thereupon the janitress made an effort to escape, but the demon barred her path, and in a sepulchral voice commanded her to go for the Mother Superior and bid her come at once, if she did not want the worst of evils to fall upon the sisterhood.

She had scarcely finished when an echoing crash was heard. The sisters suppressed a cry, and as they turned, pale with dread, before them stood their Mother Superior. With a sweeping gesture, she vaguely gave a blessing as if to endow them with courage, then turned to the janitress.

"My dear Sister Françoise, calm yourself! Be brave! God will not forsake us! I intend to comply with the desire of the stranger. I will go alone — with God alone!" Lady Beltham made a mighty effort to disguise the emotion she felt. Slowly she went down the steps and entered the sanctuary, where she halted in a state of terror.

The choir was lit up. The tapers were flaring on the high altar, and in the middle of the chapel, wrapped in a large black cloak, his face hidden by a black mask, stood a man, mysterious and alarming.

"Lady Beltham!"

At the sound of this voice, Lady Beltham fancied she recognised her lover.

"What do you want? What are you doing? It is madness!"

"Nothing is madness in Fantômas!"

Lady Beltham pressed her hands to her heart, unable to speak.

The voice resumed: "Fantômas bids you leave here, Lady Beltham. In two hours you will go from this convent; a closed motor will be waiting for you at the back of the garden, at the little gate. The vehicle will take you to a seaport, where you will board a vessel which the driver will indicate; when the voyage is over you will be in England: there you will receive fresh orders to make for Canada."

Lady Beltham wrung her hands in despair.

"Why do you wish to force me to leave my dear companions?"

"Were you not ready to leave everything, Lady Beltham, to make a new life for yourself with — him you love?"

"Alas!"

"Remember last Tuesday night at the Neuilly mansion!"

"Ah! You should have carried me off then, not left me time to think it over. Now I am no longer willing."

"You will go! Yes or no. Will you obey?"

"I will — for, after all, I love you!"

The two tragic beings were silent for a moment, listening; outside the church the uproar grew in violence, brief orders were being shouted, a blowing of whistles. Suddenly, uttering a hoarse cry, the ruffian exclaimed:

"The police! The police are on the track of Fantômas! Juve's police. Well, this time Fantômas will be too much for them. Lady Beltham — till we meet again."

Beating a rapid retreat behind a pillar of the chapel he vanished. Lady Beltham found herself alone in the chapel. Five minutes later the heavy steps of the police sounded in the passages. They went through the house, searching for clues, then disappeared in the darkness of the night.

Lady Beltham addressed the nuns:

"A great peril threatens our sisters of the Boulevard Jourdan. They must be warned at all costs and at once. And it is necessary that I, and I only, should go to warn them. Have no fear. No harm will happen to me. I know what I am doing."

Under the appalled eyes of the sisterhood the Mother Superior slowly passed from the assembled community with a sweeping gesture of farewell. The moment she was alone, she ran to the far end of the garden and passed through the little gate in the wall behind the chapel. She was gone!

While these strange occurrences were in progress at the peaceful convent of Nogent, and the flight of Lady Beltham at the bidding of Fantômas was effected under the eyes of the sisters, no little stir was manifest in the environs of La Chapelle, in the dreaded region where the hooligans, forming the celebrated gang of Cyphers, have their haunts.

A certain misrule reigned in the confederation, due to the fact that Loupart had not been seen for some time. None of its members believed for an instant the newspaper story that Loupart had turned out to be Fantômas — the elusive, the superhuman, the improbable, the weird Fantômas. This was beyond them. Good enough to stuff the numskull of the law with such a tale, but there was no use for it among the gang of Cyphers.

That same evening there was considerable excitement at the station in the Rue Stephenson. Detectives, inspectors, real or sham hooligans, were assembled there.

"Who is that gentleman?" asked M. Rouquelet, the Commissary of the district, pointing to a young man seated in a corner of the room, taking notes on a pad.

Juve, to whom the query was addressed, turned his head.

"Why, it's Fandor, Jerome Fandor, my friend."

Juve was seated at the magistrate's table, comparing papers, documents, and material evidence; he had, standing round him men in uniform or mufti. One might have thought it the office of a general staff during a battle. The door opened to a man dressed like a market gardener.

"Well, Léon?" asked Juve.

"M. Inspector, it is done. We have nabbed the 'Cooper.'"

A sergeant of the 19th Arrondissement appeared and saluted.

"M. Inspector, my men are bringing in 'The Flirt.' Her throat is cut."

"Is her murderer taken?"

"Not yet — there are several of them — but we know them. The wounded woman was able to tell us their names. They 'bled' her because they suspected her of giving us information."

M. Rouquelet telephoned to Lâriboisière for an ambulance, and the officers went to see the victim, who was lying on a stretcher in the hall. At that moment, the sound of a struggle hurried Juve to the entrance of the station. Some officers were hauling in a youth with a pallid complexion and wicked eyes. Fandor recognised the captive.

"It's that little collegian who bit my finger the night of the Marseilles Express!"

Léon, who had drawn near, likewise identified the youth.

"I know him, that's Mimile. His account is settled, he is jugged!"

The hall of the station filled once more: an old woman, dragged in forcibly, was groaning and bawling at the top of her voice:

"Pack of swine! Isn't it shameful to treat a poor woman so!"

"M. Superintendent," explained one of the men, "we caught this woman, Mother Toulouche — in the act of stowing away in her bodice a bundle of bank notes just passed to her by a man. Here they are."

The constable handed the packet to the magistrate, and Fandor, who was watching, could not repress an exclamation.

"Oh! — Notes in halves! Suppose they belong to M. Martialle! Allow me, M. Rouquelet, to look at the numbers."

"In with Mother Toulouche!" cried the Superintendent, then rubbing his hands he turned to Juve and cried:

"A fine haul, M. Inspector. What do you think?"

But Juve did not hear him; he had drawn Fandor into a corner of the office and was explaining:

"I have done no more at present than have Lady Beltham shadowed, but I do not mean to arrest her. You see, if I asked Fuselier for a warrant against Lady Beltham, a person legally dead and buried more than two months ago, that excellent functionary would swallow his clerk, stool and all, in sheer amazement."

At that moment a cyclist constable, dripping with sweat and quite out of breath, came in and hastening straight to Juve, cried:

"I come from Nogent!"

"Well?"

"Well, M. Inspector, they saw a masked man come out of the convent, wrapped in a big cloak. They gave chase — he fired a revolver twice and killed two officers."

"Good God! It was certainly — — "

"We thought, too — that perhaps — after all — it was — it was Fantômas!"

"Juve!" called the Commissary. "You are wanted on the telephone. Neuilly is asking for you."

The detective picked up the receiver.

"Hello! hello! Is that you, Michel? Yes. What is it? In a motor? Oh, you have taken the driver. But he — curse it! Who the devil is this man who always escapes us? What? He is in Lady Beltham's house! You have surrounded the house? Good, keep your eyes open! Do nothing till I come."

Juve hung up the receiver and turned to Fandor.

"Fantômas is at Lady Beltham's; shut up in the house. I am going there."

"I'll go with you."

As the two men left the station, they were met by Inspector Grolle.

"We have taken 'The Beard' at Daddy Korn's," he cried.

"Confound that!" shouted Juve, as he jumped into a taxi with Fandor. "Neuilly! Boulevard Inkermann, and top speed!"

XXXIV
FANTÔMAS' REVENGE

"Phew! Here I am!"

Checking his headlong course at the top of the terrace steps, Fantômas rapidly entered the house, then double-locked himself in. The ruffian at once inspected the fastenings of the windows and doors on the ground floor.

The monster cocked his ear. Three calls of the horn sounded dolefully in the silence of the night. Fantômas counted them anxiously and then exclaimed:

"There! That's my signal! My driver is taken."

A slight shudder shook the sturdy frame of the man. He went up to the first floor and peered through the shutters. He caught the sound of footsteps. In the light of a street lamp he suddenly descried the outline of his driver. The latter, among half a score of policemen, was walking, head bent, with his hands fettered.

"Poor fellow!" he murmured. "Another who has to pay! Ah! they have left my 'sixty horse' for my use presently. But there is no time to lose, I'll bet that Juve, flanked by his everlasting journalist, will not be long in coming here. Very well! Juve, it is not as master that you will enter this house, but as a doomed man!"

Fantômas now became absorbed in a strange task which claimed all his attention. On the floor of the dark closet where all the electric gear of the house terminated, the bandit laid a sort of oblong fusee that he drew from his capacious cloak.

He fitted to the end of this fusee two electric wires previously freed of their insulator; then having verified the tie of the pulls of the distribution board, he hid the cartridge under a little lid of wood. Then he left the closet, taking care to double-lock the door.

"These detectives," he growled, "are about to witness the finest firework display imaginable and, I dare say, take part in it, too. Dynamite can transform a respectable middle-class house into a sparkling bouquet of loose stone!"

Such was, indeed, the fearful reception Fantômas held in reserve for his opponents. He had made everything ready to blow up the house and escape unhurt himself.

If Juve and Fandor had paid more attention to the piping of the wires, they would have seen that some of them ran outside the house and disappeared below ground, reappearing at the far end of the property in an old deserted woodshed.

Fantômas was about to leave the house. He was already stepping onto the terrace when, suppressing an oath, he wheeled about suddenly.

As Juve and Fandor were about to enter the grounds, Detective Michel rose up out of the dusk.

"That you, sir?"

"Well," replied Juve, "is the bird in the nest?"

"Yes, sir, and the cage is well guarded, I assure you. Fifteen of my men kept a strict guard round the house."

"Good. Here is the plan of action. You, Sergeant, will enter the house with Inspector Michel, at my back. The men will continue to watch the exit."

Juve broke off sharply. He saw the door of the house open a little way and Fantômas appear, then vanish again inside the house.

"At last!" cried Juve, who sprang forward, followed by Fandor.

"Slowly, gentlemen! We have now victory in sight, we mustn't imperil it by rashness. You remain on the ground floor. Each one in a room, and don't stir without good reason. I am going up."

"I am going with you," exclaimed Fandor.

The two went cautiously up the stairs to the first floor.

"Fantômas!" challenged Juve, halting on the landing, "you are caught; surrender!"

But the detective's voice only roused distant echoes; the big house was silent.

"Now, this is what we must do," he cautioned Fandor. "Above us is a loft — we will search it first; if it is empty, we will close it again. Then we will come down again, taking each room in turn and locking it after us. At the slightest sound fling yourself on the ground and let Fantômas fire first; the flash of the shot will tell us where it comes from."

The two man-hunters searched the loft without success. At the first floor Juve repressed a slight tremor, for the handle of the door leading into Lady Beltham's room creaked ominously. He opened it, springing aside quickly, expecting to be fired at. The room was empty, no trace of Fantômas. The two passed into another room, then as soon as their visitation was completed locked up the apartment.

Suddenly, as they reached the foot of the stairs, Juve gave a violent start. From the door of the drawing-room a shadow, black from head to foot, came bounding out. Quick as lightning the form crossed the ante-room, then plunged by a low entrance into the cellarage.

Two shots rang out!

Fantômas drew behind him a big bar and prided himself on the barrier he thus put between his pursuers and himself. But despite his consummate confidence, he was beginning to feel a certain uneasiness, an undeniable anxiety. His black mask clung to his temples, dripping with sweat.

He crossed the basement to the little air-hole overlooking the garden.

"That is a way of escape," he thought, "unless — — "

But, baffled, he ceased his inspection.

"Curse it! There are three policemen before that exit."

He scraped a match and reviewed the place in which he found himself — which for that matter he knew better than any one.

Facing him stood the dilapidated stove and at his feet shimmered the cistern.

All at once Fantômas clenched his fists. Under the increasing blows of the detective and his men the door of the basement yielded. Above the crash of the boards and iron-work Juve's voice rang out:

"Fantômas! Surrender!"

Fantômas groped in the darkness. His hand came on a bottle. A crackle of shattered glass was heard, Fantômas had taken the bottle by the neck and broken it against the wall.

Juve, revolver in hand, followed by Fandor, moved cautiously down the stairs to the cellar: both men were brave, yet they felt their hearts beating as though they would burst.

Juve reached the last step. He pressed the knob of his electric torch; a rush of light lit up the little room. It was empty!

Juve went the round of the cellar, carefully inspecting the walls and sounding them with the butt of his revolver. He went round the cistern. Its surface was black and still. A broken bottle, floating head downward, remained half immersed, absolutely motionless.

Fandor laid his hand on the detective's arm.

"Did you hear; some one breathed!"

Beyond doubt some one had breathed!

"Idiots that we are! He is in there," cried Juve, pointing to the pipe of the great stove.

The detective caught sight in a corner of a number of bundles of straw.

"That is what we want, Fandor! We are going to make a bonfire."

When the opening of the furnace was fitted, Juve set a light to it and the flames rose, crackling, while up the pipe of the heater rose a pungent smoke, thick and black.

"And now to the openings of the stove! Sergeant! Michel! This way!"

Through the apertures in the ground-floor rooms the great stove was beginning to smoke.

A broken bottle with the bottom gone was floating head downward on the black water of the tank. Scarcely had Juve and Fandor gone than the water was stirred, and slowly the mysterious bottle rose again to the top. Behind it rose the head of Fantômas, still wrapped in the black hood which now clung to his face like a mask moulded on the features.

Dripping, he issued from the tank and breathed hard for some moments. Despite his ingenious contrivance for feeding his lungs he was not far from suffocating.

"All the same," he growled, "if I hadn't remembered the plan of the Tonkingese who lie stretched at the bottom of a river for hours at a time, breathing through hollow reeds, I think that time we should have exchanged shots to some purpose!"

Fantômas was wringing out his garments in haste when loud cries sounded above his head, and two or three shots rang out. At the same time a sudden stirring took place in and around the house. He turned it to account by going at once to the air-hole. Now there was no one on guard, so Fantômas put his head through, then his shoulders.

"That's all right; the brute is dead!"

Juve was examining curiously the creature which lay helpless on the floor. Two trembling sergeants stood at the door of the room.

"We were expecting Fantômas to appear and a snake unrolls itself and springs in our faces!" cried Fandor.

Half emerging from the mouth of the heater the monstrous body of a boa constrictor lay on the floor. The men Juve had brought into the house were resolute, ripe for anything, but never did they imagine that Fantômas could assume such an unexpected shape. And terrified, overwhelmed with dread, they recoiled in a frenzy of fear and fled, calling on their mates outside, who at once ran to their assistance.

"Sir!" A terrified voice called from outside.

Juve rushed to the window. A dripping creature, clad in black from head to foot, crossed the garden, running toward the servants' quarters. It was Fantômas. Juve swore a great oath: "There he is! Getting away!"

The detective left his cry unfinished.

As he issued by the air-holes, Fantômas leaped forward. He was free!

"Juve scored the first game, the second is mine," he cried.

He reached the woodshed. With a practised hand he turned the electric tap which ignited a spark in the dark closet behind the pantry.

"I win!" shouted Fantômas, as a terrible explosion made itself heard.

The earth shook, a huge column of black smoke rose skywards, explosion followed explosion. The roar of falling walls was mingled with fearful cries and dying groans.

Lady Beltham's villa had been blown up, burying under its ruins the hapless men who in their pursuit of Fantômas had ventured too near. Assuredly this arch-criminal had got away once more. But were Juve and Fandor among the dead?

THE END

www.ingramcontent.com/pod-product-compliance
Lightning Source LLC
Chambersburg PA
CBHW071327130626
46556CB00004B/1787